I0727431

LESLIE KOESTER

THE ANTICS of ROSE

Copyright ©2023 Leslie Koester

All rights reserved. No part of this book may be reproduced in any form or by any electronic or mechanical means, including information storage and retrieval systems, without permission in writing from the publisher, except by reviewers, who may quote brief passages in a review.

This publication contains the opinions and ideas of its author. It is intended to provide helpful and informative material on the subjects addressed in the publication. The author and publisher specifically disclaim all responsibility for any liability, loss or risk, personal or otherwise, which is incurred as a consequence, directly or indirectly, of the use and application of any of the contents of this book.

WORKBOOK PRESS LLC
187 E Warm Springs Rd,
Suite B285, Las Vegas, NV 89119, USA

Website: https://workbookpress.com/
Hotline: 1-888-818-4856
Email: admin@workbookpress.com

Ordering Information:
Quantity sales. Special discounts are available on quantity purchases by corporations, associations, and others. For details, contact the publisher at the address above.

Library of Congress Control Number:

ISBN-13:   978-1-960752-94-9 (Paperback Version)
                978-1-960752-95-6 (Digital Version)

REV. DATE: 03/03/2023

THE ANTICS OF ROSE

By Leslie Koester

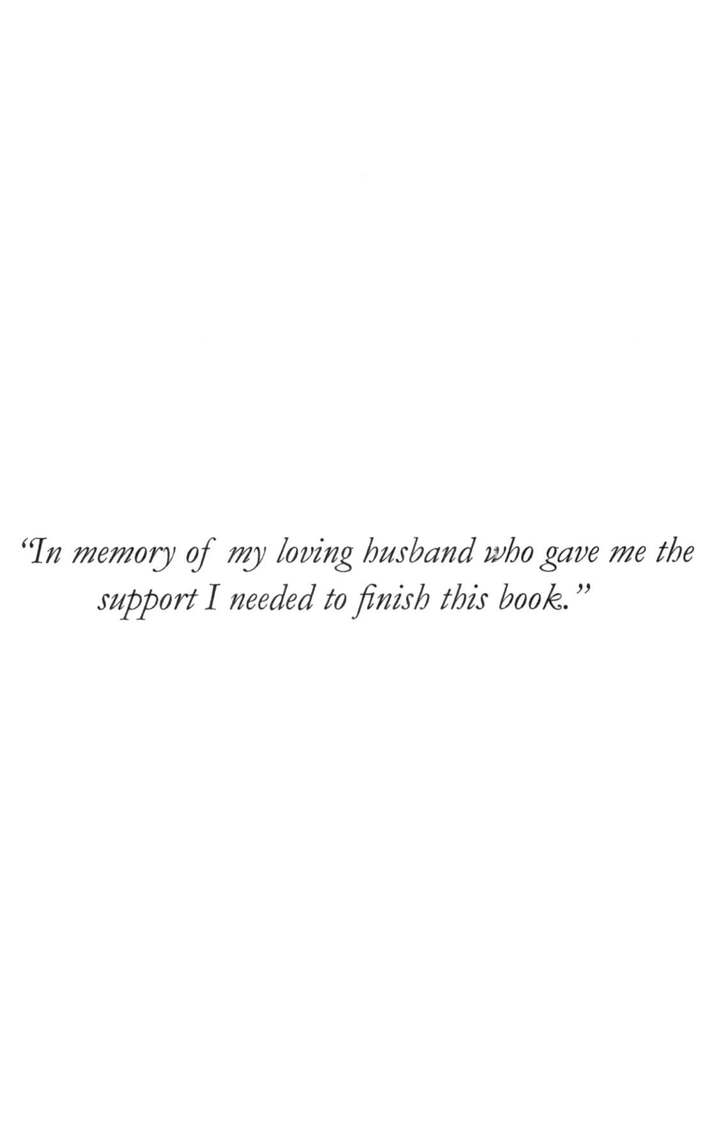

"In memory of my loving husband who gave me the support I needed to finish this book."

CHAPTER ONE

"She's doing what!" Kat dropped her head, her golden-brown hair fanning out over the top of her desk. She lifted her head up off the desk, pushing the hair out of her eyes

"Yep, you heard me, your grandma is running around outside in her bathrobe hollering for her chickens. She is insisting that the chickens need fed." Allison was trying not to bust out laughing; she could just imagine the look on her friend's face.

"Ok, I will be there in a minute." Kat sighed as she pushed end on her cell phone. She stood up cursing as her knee smacked the desk and grabbed her purse.

"Leon, I will be back later. Not sure how long I will be gone this time." Kat shook her head at the smile her Club Manager gave her.

"Grandma again?" Leon asked as he wiped the bar down.

Kat sighed, "Yes. She is running around in her bathrobe hollering for her chickens."

Leon chuckled, "I will tell Derek when he comes in later if you are not back when he gets here."

"I appreciate that. Tell him to stay out of my office or I will beat him." She said as she pushed the door open with a bang.

The gravel went flying as she stepped on the accelerator of her Mustang and headed toward her grandma's house.

#

She smiled to herself as she thought about her twin brother Derek. He meant well when he tried helping her but he just wasn't cut out for an office job. Give the guy anything electronic or with a motor and he could work wonders.

He had the same golden-brown hair as Kat but that was where their similarities stopped. While she was short and had hazel eyes that changed with her mood, he was over 6 foot with green eyes. He was always easy going and had a smile for everyone. She was usually the one that lost her temper and had little patience. Their business worked well with him handling the public and her taking care of the books.

Kat drove the five miles to her grandma's house her mind lost in thought. She barely noticed when she swerved to miss a dog in the road. Within minutes she was pulling into her grandma's driveway that she shared with Allison. The site that greeted her was her grandma standing in the front yard in her bathrobe, her face set in a stubborn scowl.

"Katherine! Thank goodness! I need to feed my chickens and this little twit won't let me!" her grandma exclaimed pointing her finger at Allison.

"Now Grandma, she is not a little twit. Be nice!" Kat smiled at her grandmother. Rosy Davis, known as Miss Rose to most of the townsfolk, could have easily passed for a woman twenty years younger. Her green eyes still appeared sharp, the laugh lines on her face apparent but not overwhelming.

"Grandma, I fed the chickens this morning before I went to work, remember?" Kat said trying to calm her grandma down; she didn't want to upset her any more than she already was. She pulled the bathrobe back up on her grandma's shoulders as it was starting to slide down and then tied it securely around the elder woman's thin waist.

At least you were able to pull her robe back up on her shoulders. She threatened to bite me when I attempted to pull it up." Allison said with a grin.

Kat's grandmother wrinkled her brow in concentration. She finally closed her eyes and shook her head. A few moments later she opened her eyes and looked at her granddaughter. "I did it again, didn't I," her grandma sighed.

"It's ok, at least you kept your clothes on this time!" Kat said smiling at her grandma as she steered her toward her house.

A while back, Allison had called Kat asking her to come help get her grandma back in the house. Miss Rose had stripped down and had went outside to take a shower in the rain. When Allison had tried to get Miss Rose to go back inside, she had just laughed at her and called her a prude. She then tried talking Allison into taking a shower outside as well. Miss Rose had later told Kat that she had done it to save on the water bill.

Her grandma just grinned, "I remember doing that!" her eyes twinkled in amusement as she remembered the shocked look on Kat's face.

Kat grinned at her grandma and just shook her head, "Grandma, what am I going to do with you?" she asked.

"Just don't put me in an old folk's home!" her grandma exclaimed. "I'm sorry you had to come out here, I should be alright now."

"Are you sure?" Kat asked dubiously, "I can stay here till Liz gets home."

"Don't you worry now Kathryn. You go on back to that club of yours. I will be just fine. Besides, this little twit," she said pointing toward Allison, "watches over me like a hawk. Can't get away with anything with her sitting in front of her window with her binoculars!"

Allison grinned at the elderly lady, "Old woman, you wouldn't know what to do without this little twit!"

"Grandma, when is Liz going to be back?" Kat asked.

Liz was Kat's cousin and had moved in with their grandmother to help keep an eye on her. Since she worked at home it was a lot more convenient for her to be around.

"She should be back soon I would think," her grandma said. "I think she had to go to Springfield for a presentation."

It never seized to amaze Kat that her grandmother could be completely off her rocker one minute and then have a better memory than anyone she knew the next.

"Ok, well I have some more bookwork to get done so I am going back to work. You don't mind keeping an eye on her for a while?" Kat asked looking at Allison.

"Of course not! What do you say old lady, you feel like playing some cards?" Allison asked Kat's grandma.

"I'm going to show you old lady you little twit! Of course, we can play some cards. I guess you're in the mood to get your butt whooped!"

Kat gave them both hugs and headed back to work.

CHAPTER TWO

Kat pulled into the club's parking lot and noticed Derek's jeep parked by the back-employee's entrance.

"If he's in my office he's had it!" she muttered out loud.

Leon gave her a knowing grin as she walked in.

"Where is he?" she said before the door closed behind her.

Leon nodded his head toward her office not saying a word but his grin got wider.

"If he has touched any of the papers on my desk Leon, I am going to beat you too!"

"Don't blame me Boss Lady! I gave him your message but he just smiled and went on in!" Leon said chuckling.

Derek was sitting at her desk with his feet propped on top of it when she walked in. He had his hat pulled down over his eyes and seemed perfectly content. He lazily pushed his hat back and smiled at her, "Hi Sis!"

"Did you mess with any of the papers on my desk?" Kat asked.

"Geez, I love you too! You could have started out with "Hi Derek! How have you been?" instead of growling at me." he said with a hurt look on his face as he got out of her chair.

"Hi Derek! How have you been? Did you mess with any of the papers on my desk?" Kat asked, this time with a smile on her face.

Derek sighed, "No, I did not mess with your paperwork. If you weren't so anal about everything I could help you more." He went and stretched his long frame out in one of the chairs in front of her desk.

Kat sighed, "I know you mean well but you help me out more by dealing with the public. I wouldn't know what to do without you and Leon here to help me out!" Kat grinned at her brother, "But, if I ever come in here and see you sitting at my desk messing with anything on it, all hells going to break loose!"

"Oh, good grief! Are you never going to stop harassing me? One little mistake and you act like the world is coming to an end!" Derek said

"One little mistake?" Kat said raising her eyebrows, "Because you are the one that ordered stock, we ran out of almost everything but Bud Light!"

Derek grinned at her, "At least we didn't run out of the good stuff!"

"Well now that is a matter of opinion." Kat grumbled and shook her head. "Was there something you was needing from me since you are in here in my domain?"

"I just wanted to give you a heads up that Blake is coming home. He should be home by the end of next week."

Kat felt a big smile light up her face, "That's great news! I will be glad to see him. It's been a while since the big lug was around."

Blake was Derek and Kat's older brother. Since he was 3

years older than the twins, he had taken it upon himself to be their protector. They really hadn't needed his protection but if anyone ever thought about giving them a hard time, one look at their brother's 6'6 frame changed their minds.

"Does Mom and Dad know he's coming?" Kat asked.

"Nope and we are not to tell them either. He is supposed to be bringing some friends with him. He wanted to make sure he was here for their anniversary."

"Well, we still have a lot to do to get their Anniversary Party ready. I have heard back from almost everyone. Only a few won't be able to make it. I have to have a ball park figure so I can get all the food and drink ordered."

"Are you going to let me help you out with that?" Derek teased.

"Well sure you can help. You just will not be allowed to do any ordering. I will need you and Blake to help with decorations."

Her brother grinned at her, "Ok. Well I guess I better get out there and see how things are going."

Kat sighed, "Yeah, I need to get this paperwork finished up."

Derek looked at his sister and got a concerned look on his face. "You know you need to slow down and have some fun. When was the last time you put yourself first instead of this place? Or when was the last time you came out and visited with everyone?"

Kat smiled at her brother, "I'm fine. I just want to make sure everything gets done before the party. This paperwork will not get done by itself."

Derek got his good-natured smile on his face. "I heard Grandma was being a handful again. Something about wanting to feed her chickens?"

Kat laughed, "She was outside in her robe and she called Allison a little twit!"

Derek started laughing, "Those two crack me up!"

Kat sat down in her chair, "It was nice to get away from here for a while. I needed a good laugh. Break time is over though, time to get back to work."

Derek sighed and looked at his sister, "You're such a slave driver!" he said as he walked out of her office.

Kat smiled as she looked down and started looking thru their inventory.

#

Derek smiled at Leon as he left Kat's office. "I guess Grandma called Allison a little twit!"

Leon started laughing, "You never know what she is going to say or do."

"The bad part is that I don't think she knows what she is going to say or do!" Derek said with a laugh.

Leon's face sobered up, "I'm worried about Kat; she is working way to hard. She is working here, planning the Anniversary Party and going to help anyone who needs her. That girl is going to run out of steam and crash!"

Derek agreed, "I told her that she needs to slow down but you know how she is. She is stubborn and will do what she wants." He got a grin on his face, "Since we all know how stubborn she is I told Blake about how she needs a break. He said when he gets home, she will slow down or he will lock himself in her office and not let her in; he knows how to do her paperwork!"

Leon got a big grin on his face, "I want to be here to watch that! When you get them two together, they bump heads and it is quite enjoyable to watch!"

"That it is!" Derek agreed.

CHAPTER THREE

"Come on Sleeping Beauty, time to get up."

Kat blinked her eyes and looked at Derek. "Huh? Oh sorry, I must have fallen asleep. What time is it?"

"You think?" Derek commented wryly. "It's 2:30 in the morning. Come on, I'll drive you home sis."

Kat groaned as she stretched her arms above her head and moved her head from side to side. "I'm ok. Just dozed off at my desk. I can drive home."

Derek started to say something but Kat held up her hand, "Don't worry. I'm done working for now. You can follow me home but I am driving my car home." she said firmly.

"Fine." Derek said with a sigh. "You really need to take some downtime. You are going to burn yourself out. If you do that then I will have to do the paperwork!"

Kat smiled tiredly at her brother, "Ok, I will sleep in and then go spend some time with Grandma. I will put off work till tomorrow afternoon. I have a lot to do but I will take a break for a while."

"Take Grandma with you. She can help get some stuff done for Mom and Dad's Anniversary Party."

Kat smiled, "I will see if she has plans. That would for sure be an adventure in itself."

Kat stood up gathering her stuff together. She stacked all of her papers together in a neat pile then grabbed her car keys out of her purse.

"Ready when you are," she said.

"Your butt is dragging and you still want to make sure your papers are all stacked in a neat little pile? Seriously! If I was you, I would just have grabbed my keys and left and worried about the paperwork tomorrow."

"That is why I take care of the paperwork. I've seen the way your apartment looks at times." Kat said laughing at her brother.

"I can tell you where everything is in my apartment." Derek said defensively. "Well at least the general vicinity of stuff anyway." He added sheepishly.

Kat and Derek walked out into the parking lot. The air was slightly cool and a slight breeze blew Kat's hair back.

"I will keep my windows down, that will keep me awake. Don't worry about following me home. I am pretty well awake now." Kat said opening her door.

"Ok, I am going on home then. I will talk to you tomorrow. Try to stay out of trouble." He said with a grin.

Kat smiled at her brother as she climbed in and started her car up. She left the parking lot and headed to her home, her thoughts already on all the stuff she had yet to do.

CHAPTER FOUR

"Well of course I can help you dear! All you had to do was ask!" her grandma told her later that day.

True to her word, Kat had drove home and went to bed. When she had woke up, she had gone outside to do some yard work after she had done some house cleaning; not that there had been a lot of work to do. She hadn't been home much to dirty anything up.

"Great, Grandma! Just let me take a shower and I will be on my way to pick you up."

"Ok dear. I will be all ready to go by the time you get here."

"Ummm, please don't wear your PJ pants and please wear a bra!" Kat pleaded.

"Alright, no PJ pants but you know my "girls" will not like being all bound up!" her grandma warned.

Kat sighed, "Just reassure your "girls" that you will unbind them when you get back home!"

Her grandma sighed but Kat could just imagine the smile on her grandma's face. "Ok, I will have regular clothes on and my girls will be where they are supposed to be."

"Thank you! I will see you in a little bit." Kat put her phone down shaking her head. It was going to be an interesting day.

An hour later Kat pulled up outside her grandmother's house.

Her grandma must have been watching for her cause she

hadn't even got out of the car and her grandma was out the door. Liz was right behind her.

"Oh, for Pete's sake!" her grandma was saying, "I will get back when I'm good and ready to get back!"

"I just want an idea as to when you will be home so I know whether or not to have something out for supper." Liz looked at Kat, "Will you two be back for supper and if so, will you be joining us?"

Kat smiled at the pleading look in her cousin's eyes. "We will probably eat out so you don't have to worry about feeding us. I will text or call you to let you know when we are heading back."

"Shouldn't matter if we are coming back here or not," her grandmother muttered, "You probably would just feed us hot dogs and macaroni and cheese anyway. Not like it would be something you would have to spend anytime fixing!"

"Grandma!" Liz exclaimed, "You act like that is all I can cook!"

"I didn't say that was all you can cook. I just said that is probably what you would fix us. Of course, with Katherine here we may have had green beans to go with it!"

"Now grandma, you know Liz takes good care of you. There is nothing wrong with hot dogs with mac and cheese for a quick meal."

"I'm ready to get out of here if you two are done ganging up on me!" their grandma exclaimed.

"Well, have a good time and I will see you when you get home." Liz said.

When Kat gave her cousin a hug, Liz whispered "Thank you! Thank you!" in her ear. Kat smiled and winked at her as she climbed in the car.

"Let's get the heck away from this funny farm!" her grandma muttered.

"You know Liz is just trying to help you." Kat said as they pulled out onto the highway.

"I know. I just get frustrated with her! She acts like I am a child and not an adult!" she sulked.

"Well, it's not like you don't push her buttons on purpose!"

"I got to get some amusement in my life!" her grandma exclaimed.

CHAPTER FIVE

Her grandma actually behaved herself for the most part. Of course, Kat hadn't expected her to behave all day.

Kat had decided to go ahead and order the food and the cake. She figured if Blake was going to show up with some of his buddies that there was not going to be any such thing as too much food.

"Well Grandma, let's go to the Party Supply store so I can pick up a few things. After that we can grab a bite to eat and then you can either go grocery shopping with me or I can take you home." Kat said.

"I'm in no hurry to get home child." her grandma said.

"Good. I'm enjoying your company." Kat said smiling.

As they pulled into the Party Supply store, her grandma got a scowl on her face. "Well, I was having a good day. Now it looks like it's about to go to pot!"

"Why is that?" Kat asked. "Ummm never mind. I see Carol's car.

Carol Huntington was around the same age as her grandmother. The two had been at each other's throats for so long that only they knew the origin of their feud-if either one of them even still remembered.

"If you want, we can go grab something to eat and then come back." Kat suggested.

"Oh no, I'm not going to leave and come back later just

because that old hussy is in there!"

With the look in her grandmother's eyes, Kat knew there was no use in arguing with her. "Just don't get us thrown out of here!" she warned.

Her grandma got a hurt look on her face, "Now I would not do anything like that!"

"Of course, you would." Kat exclaimed. "Are you allowed back in the supermarket downtown?"

"You know that was not my fault!" her grandma said.

"Oh, so the tomato threw itself at Carol's head." Kat said.

"That is exactly what happened. I tripped and the tomato fell out of my hand. Not my fault that the tomato hit her in the back of the head."

"Well, at least there are no tomatoes in the Party Supply store." Kat said.

When they first walked in Kat thought that they may actually not have a confrontation between the two ladies. Her hopes were dashed though when they turned down an aisle and a voice from behind them said "Well, I guess they let all kinds of people in here."

Kat closed her eyes and shook her head before turning around.

"Oh, dear Kat," her grandma said, "we must have walked into the wrong building! I thought they had shut all the cat houses down here in town, but she looks just like those hookers on TV!"

"Grandma!" Kat exclaimed.

Carol's smile vanished off of her face. "Your just jealous Rosy! You know I look good while you look like an old lady that has stayed out in the sun too much with no sun screen on!"

Rose sniffed, "I would much rather look the way I do than some two-bit hooker clown that hasn't realized that no man could ever get drunk enough to ever sleep with her for free let alone pay for it!"

Carol started to say something when Kat stepped in-between the two women. "You two can bicker and insult each other some other time. I got stuff to do." Kat said.

"Of course, dear!" her grandma said.

Carol said "You need to put her on a leash Katherine or leave her at home where she can have some kind of supervision. Especially if you have something to do in town. I don't see how you would even want to be seen in town with her!"

"I will make you think a leash! You're just wanting a butt whoopin' aren't you!"

"ENOUGH!" Kat said a little louder than intended. "Carol, we are here to get some stuff for my parent's anniversary. I do not have time to referee you two. Both of you need to act like adults with some sense and not talk to each other. I am going down this aisle, Carol, and you need to turn around and go the opposite way. I've seen four-year old's act better than you two."

"Your right Kat. We've got better things to do than talk to this ole bag!" Rosy made shooing motions with her hands. "You need to listen to Kat. She is irritated with both of us and is young enough to whoop both of our butts. I wouldn't mind watching you get your butt whooped, but I'm starting to get hungry and we are going to get something to eat when we leave here. Now you need to walk away before I trip and something hits you in the back of the head!"

Carol looked at both of them and then walked away without saying another word.

"Well I guess we told her!" Rosy said smiling. Her smile vanished when she saw the expression on Kat's face. "I'm sorry Kat. That woman just irks me to no end!"

Kat sighed, "It's ok Grandma At least we didn't get thrown out!"

Kat got most of the stuff for the party. The remaining decorations she needed would have to wait until she had a chance to run to one of the bigger cities close by.

"Where do you want to eat at Grandma?"

"How about Maria's Cafe?"

"Sounds good to me!" Kat said.

CHAPTER SIX

When she pulled into the cafe's parking lot, she was happy to see that there were not a lot of people there.

The door chimed as they walked into the cafe. A younger looking man looked up from a table he was cleaning. "Hello Kat and Miss Rose. You can have a seat wherever you want. I'll be right with you. Both of you want a sweet tea?"

"Of course!" they both said in unison.

The younger man brought them both their sweet teas. "You all know what you want or do I need to get you menus?"

"What's the special Kyle?" Kat's grandma asked, "How is your mother doing?"

Kyle smiled at the older woman. "The special today is lasagna, salad and garlic bread. Desserts today are bread pudding, apple cobbler or peach pie. Momma is doing just fine. I'll make sure I tell her you asked about her."

"Special sounds good to me," Kat said. "I'll take French dressing with my salad please Kyle."

"Special sounds good to me as well, but I want Ranch dressing on my salad." said Rose.

Kyle wrote down their orders and told them he would have the orders out to them as soon as possible.

Kat shook her head as she saw her grandma checking out Kyle's retreating backside. "Grandma your terrible! You are 3-4 times older than that kid!"

"Oh, for goodness sakes Katherine! I may be old but I'm not dead!"

They made small talk until their food was served. Once their food got there all conversation stopped.

"Maria's Cafe never disappoints" said Kat. "I ate too much as usual, but of course I am going to have to bring some dessert home with me."

Rose groaned, "I agree. I think Kyle is going to have to put me in a wheel barrel and wheel me out to your car!"

Kyle smiled at them as he came to their table and refilled their teas. "How was everything?"

"Fabulous as always!" Kat said with a smile.

"It was magnificent, just like the service!" Rose said.

Kyle smiled but his cheeks turned pink, "I'm glad to hear that Miss Rose".

"Kyle, can you get me some bread pudding to go? Even though I would love to sit here longer, I need to do my shopping so I can get back to work."

"Sure, thing Kat!" Kyle said.

"I do believe that boy has a crush on you Kat!" her grandma said once he was out of earshot.

"Nonsense! I'm too old for him!" Kat chuckled.

"You just don't know how beautiful you are do you?" You have admiring eyes on you all the time and you are completely oblivious!"

"Now Grandma, I never said I was ugly. I'm just puppy dog

cute!" Kat grinned. "If you see people staring this way, they are probably watching you to see what you will do next."

Kat didn't know what her grandma would have said as Kyle came back to their table with her bread pudding.

"Thanks Kyle. Did you happen to bring our ticket with you?"

"No ma'am. No ticket for you today. Both of your meals have already been taken care of." Kyle said with a smile.

"Who in the world did that?" Kat asked.

Kyle smiled, "Charlie paid for it. He said to tell Miss Rose that he would gladly take her out for dinner anytime she was willing."

Kat had to cover her mouth to stifle a laugh. "Guess we know why all those people watch us; they are actually watching you!"

"Oh, good Lord!" her grandma exclaimed. "Tell him I said not no but hell no! He thinks if he gets me to go out for dinner with him that he can get me drunk and take advantage of me! That's not going to happen!"

Kat didn't even attempt to stop the laugh that came out. Between her grandmother's outburst and the look on Kyle's face she just couldn't help herself.

"Umm do you really want me to tell him all of that Miss Rose?" Kyle stammered.

"Well of course I do..." Rose started to say.

"Not." finished Kat. "Tell him we appreciate the kind gesture and that my grandma will take his offer to heart and get back with him.

"Katherine!" her grandma spluttered, "You can't be serious...I mean when, how.... oh, good grief!"

Kyle hurried away before Rose could recover herself.

"Come on Kat, let's get out of here before he comes over here to talk to us." her grandma said standing up. Without another backwards glance she stalked to the door.

Once out in the car, Kat turned to her grandma, "You're not mad at me, are you? Charlie is not the old pervert that you make him out to be. He is one of the sweetest guys I know."

Rose sighed, "All men are nice at first, then once they get what they want or find something better they are quick to change."

Kat shook her head, "You know all men are not like that. Charlie has had a flame for you for as long as I can remember. If you didn't like him you wouldn't get all flustered every time he did something nice for you."

"I'll think about it." her grandma said, "Enough talk about matching me up to Charlie. Let's go do your shopping."

CHAPTER SEVEN

An hour and a half later they were pulling into Kat's driveway. She had not planned on being gone that long. Once they had got to the store, her grandma had stopped and talked to every Tom, Dick and Harry they had ran into. Her grandma had decided to pick up a few things as well. Her few things had turned into $100.00 worth of every little odd and end that a person could imagine.

She had tried to talk her grandma into going home first but she had told Kat that was a stupid idea. If Kat dropped her off first, she would have to back track back to her house. Made more sense for them to stop at Kat's house first to put the groceries up, bring Rose home and then Kat could go on to work.

"Kat, you really need to organize your cabinets. You should put all the soup together and then separate the canned fruits and vegetables. Also, you have several boxes of cereal and it would work better if you would put them in order of height-tallest to the shortest."

"Since I am the only one who lives here, it is not like I would have someone to move everything around to where I couldn't find stuff." Kat exclaimed.

"Dear, you never know when you may meet a guy and bring him home. What will he think when he looks in your cabinets and sees everything askew!"

"Oh, come on!" Kat exclaimed. "Can we not start talking about my lack of a love life again! I have way too much going on right now to even consider being in a relationship. Besides if I have a guy that looks in my cabinets and starts straightening everything to be in a perfect order, I would have him pushed outside of my house faster than you can shake a stick!"

Rose shook her head at her granddaughter. "Kat you have no life! You work Lord knows how many hours a day, help old ladies who are out of their head and now you are planning your parents surprise Anniversary Party! Honey you really need to go out and have some fun. When was the last time you went out on a date? Or even called one of your friends and had a girl's day?"

"What do you call what we have been doing today!" Kat exclaimed. "I have enjoyed our day together. There is never a dull moment when you are around. I wouldn't have you any other way!" Kat said as she hugged her grandma."

"Well since you're not going to let me organize your cabinets, I guess we better get going." Rose said smiling at her granddaughter.

"First your telling me that I need to stop working so hard and now your ushering me out the door! You in a hurry to get back home?" Kat teased her.

"Oh honey! I'm not going home yet. I'm going to the club with you!"

Kat looked shocked. "I thought I was taking you home. You have some groceries to put up."

"Well, I figured there is not much that needs refrigerated and you don't have much in yours so I could just leave my stuff here. I'm just not ready to go home yet. If you don't mind, I would like to go to the club and wind down a bit."

Kat sighed, "Just as long as you keep your clothes on while you are winding down this time, you can come to the club with me. You're getting too old to get on the tables."

"I'm not going to get on any tables. I can't risk falling getting down again. My ankle swelled up to the size of a Folgers coffee can and I couldn't get off the couch for a week!" her grandmother exclaimed. "I promise to keep my clothes on as well."

Kat laughed, "Ok, let's go get your stuff out of my car that needs to be refrigerated. After we get that put up, we will go to the club."

"Why do we always call it "the club" instead of its name? Grumpy's Palace is such a fun name to say!" Rose said.

"I agree, it does have a certain flare to it." Kat said smiling.

Twenty minutes later they pulled in to Grumpy's Palace. Derek's jeep and Leon's truck were already parked around back. The front of the club was already starting to fill up.

"It's not even 6 pm yet and the place is already getting busy." Kat said.

"This place is the best one around here. It's a lot cleaner than the Rabbit Hole in the next town over. Who names their establishment the "Rabbit Hole" anyway? That dump should have been called the Toilet Hole or the Sewer Stop. That's what that place reminds me of!"

"Grandma, when were you over there? You been sneaking around going to other clubs?" Kat teased.

Rose just waved her hand, "It's been a while ago. Gladys and I stopped in there to have a drink after Bingo. We walked in and then turned around and walked back out."

"That's a shame. It used to be a pretty decent place." Kat said while holding the door open for her grandma.

"Maybe if they would pay better attention to their customers like this place does, they would be a lot better place to visit." Rose said walking in thru the door.

"Miss Rose!" Leon said walking toward them, "How you been doing?"

"Hello you hunk of a man! Come here and give this old lady a hug!" Rose said smiling, "Boy you would be in a lot of trouble if I was younger!"

Leon laughed, used to the older lady's flirty banter. Derek came smiling up to them, "Grandma, don't let Cindy hear you talking like that, she's one jealous lady!"

Rose smiled at her grandson, "Hello my boy! Come and give your old grandma a hug!"

"So, what do we owe the honor of your visit Miss Rose?" Leon asked.

"She wants to wind down while I'm working." Kat said.

"Wind down? Grandma you're not going to get on any tables again, are you?" Derek said laughing.

"No, I already told Kat I wouldn't get on any tables and I would keep my clothes on. You young'uns these days just don't know how to have fun!"

Kat smiled at her grandma and told Derek to keep an eye on her while she worked. She settled in and was pleased to see that she had actually gotten more done the night before than what she thought. All she really needed to do was payroll and scheduling.

A couple of hours later she opened her office door and went looking for her grandma. It didn't take long to find her.

"Kathryn! Kat! Come over here and talk to your ole granny!" Rose hollered.

Kat walked over to her grandma. Rose was sitting at a table with several other people. "Hi Grandma. Are you enjoying yourself? How much have you had to drink?" Kat asked looking down at her grandma's half empty glass.

"Don't worry Kat. I haven't had that much to drink," her grandma told her and then let out a loud belch. Rose looked startled, as if she couldn't believe that sound had come out of her. "Oh, my goodness! Excuse me!"

Kat raised her eyebrows at her. "Well, that's reassuring, I'm glad to hear that. No dancing on the tables? I see you still have your clothes on."

"I told you that I wasn't going to get on the tables and that my clothes would stay on. To tell you the truth I'm getting a little tired. I think I will finish this drink and then have you take me home, if you don't mind."

"Sure, I can do that. What are you drinking anyway? Is that vodka and 7-up?"

"Well of course it is! You should sit down and have one with me."

"If I have a drink, it won't be that! I think I will have an Amaretto Stone Sour."

"One Amaretto Stone Sour coming up!" Kat heard a voice behind her say. She turned around as Derek came up to her. "I'm glad to see you out of your cave sis. What brings you out here to mingle with us peasants?" he teased.

Kat smiled, "I am actually pretty well caught up for tonight. I have a delivery tomorrow that I need to be here for but thought I would come out and be sociable."

"Well, why don't you have a seat next to Granny and I will go get your drink. Anyone else need anything?"

"If you don't mind, I will take another beer," said Grant who was sitting next to her grandma. Grant had gone to school with their parents and had always been a close family friend.

"Sure thing. If no one else needs anything, I will be right back." No one else needed anything so Derek headed up to the bar.

Kat settled down next to Rose. She looked around the club and smiled. It had been awhile since she had been out there for anything other than business.

She smiled and waved at several people. A few came up and asked her how she had been.

Derek came back with her drink and Grant's beer. Kat took a sip and sighed. She couldn't remember the last time she had a drink and just sat down to relax. "This tastes wonderful! You never disappoint me when you make me a drink."

"Well you know the rules, if you have more than a couple drinks, we get your keys. Doesn't matter if you own this place or not!" Derek said firmly.

Kat had decided to employ several people to act as designated drivers. No one ever went by themselves when taking customers home; it was at least two people that went. They knew most of the people that came in. Being a small town, they knew where most of the locals lived. One person would drive the customer's car to their house while the other person would drive another car and follow them. Once at the customer's house both employees would help the person in and then lock up when they left after they had the person all settled in.

"I'm only going to have this one drink," Kat reassured him.

"Kat, when are you going to get yourself a man?" Grant asked her. "You're a beautiful girl, you look a lot like your mother. Any man would be lucky to have you."

"I agree. When are you going to get you a man?" Derek smirked.

"Don't you have work to be doing?" Kat asked him.

"Umm, nope don't think so. I'm pretty good friends with the owner so I get some slack."

"Oh really? Well I'm gonna have to have a talk with the owner then. Can't have slackers running around here." Kat teased.

"Well Kathryn? Don't try changing the subject. When are you gonna get yourself a man? Make sure you get one worth a damn. I think you should have me meet them before you get serious, to get my stamp of approval. I can get a questionnaire made up for him to fill out and have him strip down for a physical!" Rose said.

"Oh my, Grandma your terrible!" Kat laughed "Thank you for the offer but I wouldn't want you to go to all that trouble for me."

"No trouble at all! I would be happy to help you out!" her grandma said winking at her.

Raised voices got Kat's attention. Derek muttered under his breath as he looked towards the bar.

"Now what's going on?" Kat asked.

Derek sighed, "Well, Melissa's old man Rick has been in here the last couple of weeks. He's been getting pretty friendly with Hope. Looks like Melissa found him and all hell's going to break loose."

Derek started heading that way. Kat got up to follow him. Leon had already got to Melissa and was trying to get her to calm down.

"You're a pathetic excuse of a man!" Melissa was saying as Kat and Derek got up to them.

"Is he pathetic, or are you? He is obviously not getting what he needs at home, which is why he's here with me." Hope said.

Rick just kept on drinking his beer watching the two women.

Derek went over to get in front of Hope, who had jumped up out of her chair. Kat had not realized her grandma had followed both of them up to the bar until she heard her voice behind her.

"Are you kidding me, you little floozy! You're up here almost sitting on a married man's lap; that's pretty pathetic in my eyes. What's the matter with you? Can't you get your own man?" Rose stormed.

"Why don't you go back to your rocking chair old lady. This is none of your concern!" Hope fumed.

Kat looked at Rick, who was still watching all the drama unfolding while drinking his beer. From out of nowhere a shoe went flying by her head and hit Hope in the chest.

"Grandma!" Kat exclaimed.

"You old senile witch! What is wrong with you?" Hope hollered.

"Well, you know how us old women get! If I'm going back to my rocking chair, I'm gonna get comfortable!" Rose said taking her other shoe off. Kat grabbed the shoe before it could be launched at Hope as well.

"Grandma, go back to the table. You're just going to make things worse."

"You sure you don't need me to help out? I could help keep the peace." Rose said.

"No Grandma. You're just getting them wound up." Kat handed her grandma her shoes back. "Now take your shoes and go back to the table." Kat said firmly. Rose looked at Kat's face and nodded, "Fine, but if you need me just holler!"

Kat watched her grandma head back to her table and shook her head. Behind her Derek and Leon were still trying to calm the girls down. Rick was still sitting down drinking his beer. Kat looked at Rick, "So, what do you think about all of this Rick?"

Rick put his beer down and looked at the girls. The girls had stopped arguing when they heard Kat ask Rick her question. Derek and Leon both looked at Kat expectantly, both wondering why she would ask that question. Rick cleared his throat and reached for his beer. Both of the girls looked at Rick waiting on his reply.

After taking a long swig he put the bottle back on the table and cleared his throat again. When he went to reach for his beer again Melissa snapped "You grab that beer again mister and you will be wearing it!" Hope smirked and said "We agree on that!"

Rick sighed, "Well how about them Cubbies! You think they will go all the way again this year?"

Derek started laughing and both of the women started hollering again. "You need me to come back over there?" her grandma hollered.

"Nope, we got it under control Grandma." Derek hollered back at her.

"Doesn't look like it from over here," their grandma said.

Kat sighed and tried again. "Rick you have a big problem right now. You're a married man who has been spending a lot of time with another woman. Your wife just walked into my club and is now standing by your table. The woman you're with is saying stuff to your wife and making matters worse. Now your gonna leave your beer on the table and you're going to explain to both of these women what the hell is going on. If any of you three raise your voices again and disrupt my club, a side of me that is not very nice is going to come out and lay the smack down on all of ya!"

Rick's jaw dropped and his eyes widened. Both of the women looked at Rick.

"That's my girl!" Rose hollered. "You tell them how it is!"

"It's not going to do me any good to speak. As soon as I start talking, one or both of them are gonna start interrupting me to get their two cents in."

Kat looked at the two women, "He is going to talk and you two are going to keep your mouths shut."

"This may be your club but you can't make me keep my mouth shut!" Hope said.

"Your right, I can't make you keep your mouth shut, but this is my club and I can throw your ass out!"

Rick looked at Melissa, "First of all, I haven't had sex with Hope. I've been coming in here to get out of the house. You have been very moody lately and have been acting like you don't want me around. I admit I enjoy the attention that Hope has been giving me, but I do love you and I wouldn't cheat on you." Rick looked at Hope, "I'm sorry if I have been leading you on. That wasn't my intention."

"You're kidding, right? We've been spending all this time together and it didn't mean anything to you?" Hope said disbelief in her voice.

"I'm sorry." Rick said again.

"Time for you to leave floozy!" Rose said from behind Kat.

Kat turned around and looked at her grandma, "Didn't I tell you to stay at your table?"

"Well, if you all hadn't lowered your voices, I wouldn't have had to come over here to hear what was being said!" Rose said.

"Old lady, I've had about enough of you!" Hope said getting back out of her seat.

Melissa looked at Rick, "I'm sorry if I have been acting that way. I've had a lot on my mind. That is still not an excuse to be up here spending that much time with her." she said pointing at Hope.

Hope looked at Melissa, "He can say whatever he wants. The truth is if you hadn't come in here tonight, he would have taken me home and I would have given him some attention!"

"You're crazy!" Rick said.

"I knew you were a floozy but I didn't think you were that stupid! Rick, what is wrong with you! I think if I was you, I would rather be home with Melissa no matter how moody she gets than be up here with this fake ho!" Rose said.

"That's it! Old lady you better shut your mouth or I will shut it for you" Hope said.

Kat looked at Hope, "That is my Grandma your talking to so you better watch it!"

"That's it Kat, you take care of my light work for me!" Rose said.

Hope lunged toward Rose but Derek grabbed her before she got very far.

"Derek, get her ass out of here. Call her a cab. Hope, the next time you come here you better act like you haven't lost all of your common sense or I will make sure you don't come back in here at all." Kat said.

Derek grabbed Hope's arm and started walking her towards the front door. "Actually, Derek and I can run her home. We are on "cab duty" tonight." Leon said, "That is if you can handle everything while we are away."

"Of course, she can! I'm here to help her and we can manage without you two!" Rose said.

Leon looked at Kat and raised his eyebrows. "We'll be fine. You just get her home and get back here as soon as you can." Kat said reassuringly. "Come on Grandma, let's get you back to your table." Kat said holding on to her grandma so she couldn't wonder away.

"Kat, as soon as the boys get back, I'm wanting to go home. It's been a long day for me."

"Rose, I'm almost done with my beer. I can take you home." Grant offered.

"How many beers have you had Grant?" Kat asked.

"The last drink your brother brought me was the second one of the night." Grant said.

"We'll be fine dear. I will talk to you tomorrow when you bring me my groceries."

"I'm not sure when I'll be by Grandma." Kat said.

"Whatever time you get there Kathryn will be fine." Rose reassured her.

"Are you going to finish your drink before I take you home Rose?" Grant asked.

"Well, of course I am. What a stupid question, Grant!" Rose scolded him. "Kat you may as well finish your drink too."

Kat sighed, "I better not. I need to go help Megan up at the bar. Looks like she is getting quite the crowd up there. Grant, take care of my Grandma. Grandma, behave yourself and get some sleep. I love you and will see you tomorrow." Kat said giving her grandma a kiss on the cheek and a quick hug.

"I love you too. Don't worry about me. Grant will take good

care of me. Rose picked up her glass and drained the rest of it. She put the glass down on the table with a bang, "That sure did taste good. If your done Grant we can go ahead and leave."

"You're the boss Rose, whatever you say goes. Talk to you later Kat."

CHAPTER EIGHT

Kat headed up to the bar to help Megan out. She had just hired her about 5 months ago, just to help fill in every once in a while, but the girl was doing a great job. Megan shot Kat a grateful look. "Thanks for coming to my rescue Kat. Sorry you're not getting to relax."

"No worries Megan. You're doing a great job." Kat told her, "Don't take any crap from these guys and you will be fine."

"Where you been all my life sweetheart?" an old man by the name of Stewart asked Megan as he grabbed her arm. Kat tried to keep an eye on what was going on in case Megan needed her.

"Hello Stewart, same answer as all the other times you've said that to me." Mega said as she took Stewart's hand off of her "I was either not thought of, in my momma's belly or in school."

Several of the patrons started laughing, Stewart himself being one of them. "Well maybe I'm just gonna keep asking you till you change your answer." he said.

"Give it up Stu! She's trying to tell you that you are way too old for her and you don't stand a chance!" Danielle, one of the other patrons hollered from the end of the bar.

"You never know! Maybe one of these days she will change her mind and see that I am her Prince Charming!"

Kat smiled at Megan, "Great job! You handled that very well. Stewart can be a handful but he wouldn't hurt a fly."

The two women worked together behind the bar as if they had done it a hundred times before. They made small talk with each other and with the patrons sitting at the bar. Kat found herself enjoying being out of her office and among the people in her club.

"I am going to walk around and ask everyone how they are doing and if they need anything. Think you can handle this for a while by yourself?" Kat asked Megan.

Megan looked over at Kat, "If not then you will hear me hollering for you" she joked. Megan's brown eyes sparkled as she looked at Kat and pushed her dark hair back behind her ears.

"I'll be fine. Go and enjoy yourself."

Kat grabbed a little notebook that was behind the bar and went around asking customers if they needed a refill and asking them how their families were. Several of them exclaimed how happy they were to see her and asked how her parents were doing. A few of them asked how the Anniversary Party planning was coming along and if there was anything they could do to help.

"You just let me know if there is anything I can do to help you out sweetheart. If you decide you need someone to bring in food or help decorate, you just let me know!" Myrtle White said at a table Kat stopped at.

Myrtle was in her 70's and was one of the best cooks in town. On occasion she would bring in homemade desserts to Marie's Café to sell. As soon as word got out that she had been baking, most of the town would show up to get some of the heavenly treats that she had made.

"I can see you making food for the party, but there is no way that you would be able to help decorate. You won't be able to climb up on the ladders!" Jenny said.

Myrtle and Jenny had been friends for a long time; they were closer than sisters.

"I don't need to climb on any ladders. I am sure Kat will have tables that need decorating." Myrtle said looking at her friend.

"I will let you know if I need any help. I appreciate your offer Myrtle." Kat said.

"Of course, you can always count on me to help too Kat. I at least can climb ladders." Jenny chimed in.

"You can't climb ladders any more than I can. If you were to try to climb a ladder, you would fall and break your fool neck!" Myrtle chortled.

The two ladies started arguing over who would be the best one to help Kat decorate for the party. Kat took that opportunity to head back up to the bar to get the few drink requests she had been given while making her rounds.

"Everything going ok?" Kat asked Megan as she came back around the bar.

"Everything is just fine." Megan said as she got Stewart another beer.

"One of these days Kat, I am going to wear Megan down." Stewart said earnestly.

"Well, I guess you can just keep trying Stu, but I must admit I am a little jealous. You used to try to be my Prince Charming." Kat said looking at the older man sadly.

"Oh no, honey, you know I still love you! I can be both of you princess's Prince Charming!" Stu said beaming and taking Kat's hand in his own.

"You are so full of horse shit! You wouldn't be able to handle one of them little ladies, let alone both of them." Danielle smarted off, "They would probably give you a heart attack."

"At least I would die with a smile on my face," Stewart said grinning.

CHAPTER NINE

Leon and Derek came walking up. "Got that little hellcat home. Only a few battle scars." Leon said to Kat as he pointed at Derek. Kat looked over at her brother and gasped. His arms were covered with bloody scratches. "She caught me unaware." he mumbled.

"Geez Derek! Let's go to my office and get you cleaned up." Kat said grabbing his arm and yanking him towards her office.

"Ow! Easy! I'm damaged merchandise!"

"Oh, quit your whining. Sit down so I can clean you up. You never know what kind of germs that woman could have had on her hands and under her nails!"

Megan popped her head in Kat's office. "Kat, Grant's on the phone for you."

"Tell him I will call him back in a little bit."

"I think you better take this. He says it's about Miss Rose."

"Oh Lord! What has she done now? Megan can you finish cleaning Derek up?"

"Sure." Megan said smiling at Derek.

"Hello Grant. What has she done this time?" Kat said.

"Well, promise me you won't get mad at me," Grant started, "but your grandma is hanging out the basement window and refuses to let me or Liz get her back in."

"She's what? It sounded like you said Grandma was hanging out a window and she is refusing to let you or Liz help her in."

Derek and Megan started laughing. "This is a new one, even for her!" Derek said.

"Why is she hanging out the window?" Kat asked in disbelief.

"Well, when I went to drop her off Liz came storming out of the house. She was mad because you hadn't texted her to let her know what was going on. She really blew up when she got close enough to your Grandma to smell the whiskey on her breath. She told Miss Rose to get in the house. Of course, you can imagine how that went over." Grant said.

"Ok, so how did she end up hanging out the window?" Kat asked sighing.

"Well, after her and Liz exchanged some words Miss Rose said she wanted me to take her back here. Liz disagreed and started growling at me. Miss Rose went inside and we didn't think anything of it; that is until she started hollering. We both went around the house and she was hanging out the basement window. Every time we go to help her, she either starts swinging or kicking at us. Liz and I both thought maybe you could come over here and try talking to her."

"Alright, I will be right there." Kat sighed as she hung up the phone. "Megan can you finish cleaning Derek up? Make sure you put some antibiotic cream on it as well."

"If you hang on a minute, I can go with you." Derek offered.

"You need to get cleaned up. When you get done here you can come on out if you want. I'm probably going to go on home after I deal with this."

"Alright, be careful. You want Megan to leave the first aid kit out? Just in case?" Derek said only half teasing.

Kat sighed, "Might be a good idea." She waved at them as she went out the door.

Five minutes later she was pulling in her grandma's drive. She could hear her grandma hollering as soon as she opened her car door.

"I am not going to tell you two again! Get away from me. I will get out of this window when I'm good and ready! I'm an adult. If I want to hang out my own damn window then I'm going to!"

"Grandma, why are you hanging out your window?"

"Hello Kathryn. How's the club going? Get that crazy ole ho home?" Rose said, as if she wasn't hanging out the window.

"Yes Grandma. Derek and Leon got her home. Derek came back with some battle scars. She scratched up his arms pretty good."

"Just wait till I see that little slut! I will tear her apart for putting her hands on him!"

"Well Grandma, it will be kind of hard to "tear her apart" when your hanging out the window."

"I know I look silly, hanging out my window. I don't know why they made this window so far off the ground."

"Maybe they had little ole ladies that liked to try to sneak out of their own house by going down into the basement and trying to crawl out the window!" Liz said.

"You need to respect your elders Elizabeth!"

"Well maybe if my elder wasn't hanging out the window drunk, I would be able to respect her more!" Liz reported.

"Liz, I could really use a cup of coffee if you don't mind getting me one." Kat asked looking at her cousin.

Liz turned around without saying another word and headed back into the house.

"Ok Grandma, you want to tell me why you are hanging out the basement window?"

"I get so tired of being treated like a little kid. Telling me to go in the house and that I couldn't go back to the club! I just kind of lost it for a minute. I just wanted to go back to the club where everyone treated me like an adult and not a child. Now I really want to go back to the club for another damn drink!"

"Will you let me help you out of the window?" Kat asked.

"I would have been ok if the damn stool I was standing on hadn't fell over when I went to crawl out the window! Then my dog-gone britches got caught on something and I am actually not able to get out." Rose said sheepishly.

"Hi Grandma! How the hell are ya?" Derek's voice came from behind Kat. "You know if you wanted to go star gazing there are easier ways to go about it!"

"Derek, can you go down into the basement and help me with getting Grandma back in?" Kat asked.

"Sure, I can hold onto her while you get her unstuck." Derek said.

"You sure you can hold onto me with your battle scars?" Rose asked.

"You just had to tell her didn't you!" Derek said looking at Kat. "I'll be fine Grandma; I've had worse battle scars."

"I am sure scratches from a woman are usually given to you under a lot funner circumstances!" Rose said smiling.

Derek laughed, "Oh yeah! This one chic a while back tore me up pretty good but man was it worth it!"

"That's my boy!" Rose said.

"Can we get on with this?" Kat said.

"I hope you tore her up some too!" Rose giggled.

"Oh, good Lord you two! I really don't want to stand here listening to Derek's sex stories while you encourage him and tell him what a good job he's doing!"

"I'm going! Geez sis, you're just jealous cause you haven't been "tore up" for quite some time!"

"Derek! My sex life is none of your business! Now get downstairs!" Kat said cheeks blazing.

A short time later they were trying to get Rose unstuck.

"Don't you two tear my britches any more than what they already are! Watch my girls! I don't want them smashed or one to get longer than the other one with you two pulling and pushing me!"

"Grandma, can we please not talk about your girls!" Derek groaned.

"Oh, it's ok to talk about your sex stories but we can't talk about my girls! How selfish you are!"

"I would rather not hear about either one of them!" Kat

said, "Almost got her undone. Grandma, lean to your left a bit.... gotcha!"

Rose disappeared back into the basement.

Kat went around to the front of the house and went inside. As soon as she got inside, she could hear voices coming from the kitchen.

Liz's angry voice rang out as Kat stepped into the room, "I'm tired of you treating me like crap!"

"You are such a drama queen!" Rose snapped, "You're living under my roof, rent free, and only have your own bills to pay. You're pretty ungrateful if you ask me!"

"Ungrateful! Are you kidding me! I moved in here with you to help take care of you. Someone needed to be here in case you went all crazy again!" Liz fumed.

"Maybe I'm all crazy cause you're living here treating me like a child!"

"Well maybe if you didn't act like a child you wouldn't be treated like one!" Liz countered.

The two women were standing in the middle of the kitchen. Derek and Megan were leaning against the counter and Grant was sitting at the kitchen table drinking a cup of coffee.

"There's a fresh cup of coffee sitting on the counter for you Kat." Grant said taking a sip.

Kat sighed, "Maybe one of you should come home with me tonight and then you two can talk tomorrow."

Rose said "Well even though this is my house, I'll go home with you Kathryn. I need to get away from this looney toon for a while!"

"Well, I'm sure not going to stop ya! Besides, if I left someone else would have to stay here with your crazy ole ass!"

"That's enough you two! It's late and I want to go home. Grandma, go get you an overnight bag." Kat said. "I'm so glad you all were in here keeping control of the situation. Whatever would I do without you," she said wryly after her grandma left the room.

Derek shrugged, "I wasn't going to get in the middle of them. If it got physical, then I may have stepped in-between them."

"Oh, good grief! I wouldn't have gotten physical with Grandma! She irritates me but I would never put my hands on her. Give me some credit!" Liz said.

"I wasn't talking about you getting physical with Grandma, I was talking about Grandma getting physical with you!" Derek said smirking.

"Lucky you Megan! Welcome to our crazy family! Why did you come here with Derek anyway?"

Kat asked.

"Well open your eyes Kathryn! Anyone can see that they are an item. You two porkin' yet?" Rose asked with a devilish grin on her face as she walked into the room.

Derek grinned really big while Megan's cheeks got red."

"Good Lord Grandma!" Kat said. She looked at Derek and Megan and blinked. "Sorry you two, guess I just didn't notice. Derek, she's a good one, better hang on to her! You better treat him right too! I like you Megan and I know he can be a cocky jerk at times but he is still my brother."

"How many times do I got to tell you-I'm confident not cocky!" Derek argued.

"Whatever! You know I'm right but you can stay in denial if you want. Grandma, you ready to get out of here? I'm tired."

"I'm all ready to go Kathryn." Rose looked over at Liz, "Don't have any wild parties while I'm gone," she warned.

"I'm not going to have a party! I'm just going to enjoy the peace and quiet with you gone!"

Kat shook her head at her cousin as she herded her grandma out the door.

CHAPTER TEN

After Kat and Rose left, Derek started laughing. "Do you think Kat suspects anything?"

Liz smiled, "Nope, I don't think she does. It's all up to Grandma now. You think she can keep her busy tomorrow?"

"Well, if anyone can, Miss Rose can do it!" Grant said.

"How did Blake know she would want to take one of us home?" Liz asked.

"Blake knows us better than we know ourselves. He grew up taking care of us. He knows that Kat likes to keep the peace. Besides we had Plan B in case we needed it." Derek said.

Megan looked at the other three, "Wait a minute, this was all to get Kat to take Miss Rose home with her? You two weren't really arguing? Miss Rose was not actually stuck in the window?"

"Nope, our arguing was fake but her getting stuck was real enough." Liz said smiling.

"But why go to such lengths?" Megan asked puzzled. "If you wanted Miss Rose to stay at Kat's house, I am sure all you would have had to do was just ask her!"

Derek looked over at her, "What fun would that have been? Blake called me while she was in her office. He will be here tomorrow evening with some of his friends. Grandma's going to keep Kat busy so he can surprise her. Kat is supposed to be at work tomorrow between 10:30 and 11:30 for a delivery.

Grandma is going to talk her into going to town to get the rest of the party stuff. Blake and his buddies are going to be in Kat's house when they get back. She doesn't know it yet but she is going to be having house guests until the party!" he said grinning.

"So, Blake and his friends are going to stay at her house and she doesn't know it? Oh Wow! She is going to come unglued. Why are they staying at her house and not yours?" Megan asked.

"Because I have a sex life and she doesn't" he said pulling Megan into his arms.

"You are terrible!" Megan said.

"Well that is part of it anyway. Kat's house is big. She has three extra rooms upstairs and three bedrooms downstairs, including her own. I only have one extra room. I have people coming and going all the time while she lives outside town surrounded by woods and a pond. If they stay at her house it is less likely that they will be seen." He exclaimed.

"Well that does make sense." Megan agreed and then gasped when Derek started kissing her neck.

"Would you two mind leaving before you start taking each other's clothes off? I'm ready for bed!" Liz said rolling her eyes.

"Me too!" Derek said smiling at Megan.

Grant started laughing "I'm headed home too. Good night everyone."

CHAPTER ELEVEN

"Good grief Grandma! What all did you put in here?" Kat said as she put her grandmother's suitcase in her trunk.

"Just normal stuff," her grandma shrugged.

"Grandma, do you have glass in here? I could have sworn I heard glass clink together." Kat said.

"Well I imagine that is probably my perfume bottles." Rose said.

"Bottles? Why would you have more than one? You do realize that I am bringing you back home, tomorrow right?" Kat said.

"Well, I know that is the plan but I figured if we end up going out of town tomorrow to finish picking up stuff for your parent's party, I better have an extra set of clothes for church on Sunday in case we get back late and I stayed at your house again."

"What does having an extra set of clothes do with having your suitcase make clinking sounds? Why would you need more than one bottle of perfume?"

"Well, that sound could have also been from the bottle of vodka in there too," her grandma said matter-of-factly.

"You weren't even gone 10 minutes! How did you get your suitcase packed that fast and have time to pack a bottle of vodka as well!" Kat asked in amazement.

"Honey, when you get my age you know how to pack the important stuff!" her grandma said, obviously proud of herself.

"And you think that vodka is one of the "important stuff" that you need to pack when spending the night with your granddaughter? What is wrong with you? We really need to have a talk about your priorities and probably get you to an AA meeting!"

"Of course, it is important! How do you expect me to drink my orange juice in the morning without my Vodka!"

"Why would you be drinking vodka with orange juice first thing in the morning?" Kat gasped.

"Well how else am I supposed to put up with your cousin! You live with her for a while and let's see if you don't start having vodka with your orange juice!" her grandma snapped.

Kat sighed as they pulled in to her drive. The site of her house welcomed her as did the automatic lighting that came on when she opened her garage door."

"Ok Grandma, let's get you all settled in," she said as she opened her car door.

"Of course, dear. Thank you for taking care of me."

"No problem," she said as she hefted her grandma's suitcase out of the trunk.

Once inside Kat took the suitcase to one of her spare rooms downstairs. "Well you know where everything is, make yourself at home. I am going to bed and I will talk to you in the morning." She said as she kissed her grandma on the cheek and hugged her. Her grandma gave her a kiss and hug back, thanked her again and said good night.

Kat went into her own room, took a shower and climbed into bed. Within minutes she was sound asleep.

CHAPTER TWELVE

You're kidding me! Miss Rose actually packed vodka to go spend the night at your house. Did you have the OJ to go with it?" Leon asked.

Kat had come in fairly early and had been telling Leon about everything that had happened the night before. Leon had almost lost his breath laughing so hard when she had told him about Rose getting stuck trying to crawl out the window.

"Oh yeah, she knew I had orange juice because she was with me when I got it." Kat shook her head, "She was actually up before I was this morning. She was washing her bed sheets of all things. It was pretty nice having her around. She even had breakfast made for me!"

"Oh yeah? That was pretty nice of her. Did she happen to give you vodka in your orange juice too?" Leon asked with a twinkle in his eye.

"As a matter of fact, she did! She had made me a scrambled egg omelet and toast. When I went to take a drink of my OJ, I wasn't expecting to taste vodka in it!" Kat said laughing. "She then told me I was being a big baby and to suck it up because it would make my day better!"

Leon got to laughing so hard he had tears going down his face. "You never know what she is going to do or say. She is a riot! Where is she now?"

"She is still at my house. She wasn't ready to go talk to Liz yet so I told her she could stay at my house. I told her not to get too drunk and drown in my hot tub!" Kat started laughing again.

Both of them were still laughing when Roger, the delivery man showed up. "You two been in the booze this morning already?" he asked.

Leon, still laughing, said "As a matter of fact Kat had vodka in her OJ this morning!"

"Wow Kat! I never thought of you as a closet morning boozer!" he said smiling.

Kat laughed, "Normally, I'm not! Grandma spent the night last night at my house. Apparently, she thinks having vodka and OJ in the morning makes your day better!"

"Now that I can believe! How is Miss Rose doing anyway?"

"She is doing just fine. I guess after I get done here, we are going to Terra Haute or Champaign to a Party Supply store to finish getting stuff for Mom and Dad's Anniversary Party. You still planning on being there? Blake is supposed to be here for it and I am sure he would love to see you. He is supposed to be bringing some friends of his along too." Kat said.

Blake and Roger had gone to school together and had gotten into all kinds of mischief. Kat and Blake's dad had bailed the two out of jail a couple of times but the charges were always dropped. Neither one of them knew how to keep their mouths shut, especially when liquor was involved. This had been a problem when guys from one of the other towns had come looking for trouble. They figured if they were coming to them looking for trouble, they were going to oblige them.

"It would be nice to see him again. He bringing that goofy guy he had with him last time? What was his name…William, Larry or something like that?" Roger asked.

"Are you talking about Reggie? The guy with the red hair? The one that followed Allison around like a little puppy?" Kat asked.

"That's the one! He's not very bright, is he?" Roger said.

"Oh, he's smart enough, just not much on common sense. You should be ashamed of yourselves, taking him Snipe hunting! Poor city boy!" Kat said laughing.

"Snipe hunting? Seriously! I thought everyone knew what Snipe hunting is!" Leon said.

Roger smiled, "That was pretty fun though! You should have seen his face. Blake and I had night vision goggles on watching him. We were following him and intentionally making noise. Got to give the guy credit, he only screamed like a girl once and that was at the end when Blake threw that stuffed raccoon at him!"

Leon started laughing, "That's why I am not going anywhere. I love my job and there's never a dull moment around here. Not to mention that most people around here would do anything for a person."

"Not to mention Cindy would never leave here." Kat chimed in.

"True, she doesn't even like going to town. She said that if our town does not have what she wants then it is something that she doesn't need." Leon said smiling thinking about his wife.

Kat's cell phone started ringing, when she looked and seen who was calling, she groaned, "Grandma's calling; wonder if she is out of vodka?" she said before answering.

"Kathryn? Are you almost done?" Rose asked.

"Almost Grandma. You ok?" Kat said a little concerned.

"Well of course I am! Derek called me to ask how I was feeling. I told him I was feeling just fine. He said he was getting ready to go to your club so I asked him to come get me so you wouldn't have to come back home to get me before we headed to town."

"It's not that big of a deal Grandma. I don't mind coming home to get you. Derek doesn't need to come get you." Kat protested.

"Oh, he doesn't mind! Besides he is taking me muddin before we go there. I asked him if I could drive and he had the balls to tell me no!" Rose grumbled.

Kat had her phone on speaker so both guys heard what Rose said.

"Now Miss Rose, you just need to get your own jeep or big truck so you can go muddin!" Roger said.

"Is that you Roger? Boy, I haven't seen you in a coons age! How you been? How's that beautiful family of yours?" Kat's grandma asked.

"Everyone's doing good. Katie lost her first tooth the other day. We had a heck of a time getting her to go to bed. She was determined to stay up and give the tooth to the tooth fairy herself because she wanted to make sure that her tooth was going to be taken care of. She said if they were going to throw her tooth away then she wasn't going to let them have it even if they gave her a gazillion dollars." Roger said chuckling. "Her brother Jeff told her that her tooth would go to other kids who were sick and lost their teeth. That made her feel better so she decided she better get to sleep cause some kid was probably waiting on her tooth."

"Now isn't that something! Your kids sound wonderful. You will need to bring them over sometime." Rose said.

"I will make sure I do that Miss Rose." Roger said.

"How long you going to be gone muddin Grandma?" Kat asked.

"Well, that's why I'm calling you honey. Derek is on his way now. I was wanting to know how long you are going to be so I can tell Derek how long we can be gone."

"Well, Roger just got here. We've been talking and haven't gotten down to business yet. I am sure I can find something to do until you get here. Just as long as you aren't gone all day! If anything, I will just go on home and wait on you to get done." Kat said.

"No sense doing that Kathryn. If you run out of things to do just call me and I will have Derek bring me on in. That way you're not wasting gas." Rose said.

"It's not that big of a deal Grandma. Not like I'm an hour away. You just have fun and if I get tired of waiting on you, I will call you to let you know I'm heading home." Kat told her.

"Ok Kat. I think Derek just pulled down your drive so I'm going to go. Don't forget to call me when you get tired of waiting on me though. I would hate for us to miss each other." Rose said.

"Ok Grandma. I will let you know. You have fun and I will see you later. Love you and be careful." Kat said.

"Ok honey. I love you too. You boys be good and I will talk to you soon." Rose said.

"Bye Miss Rose." Roger and Leon both said.

Kat hung up her phone and looked at Roger. "Guess it's time to get back to work if you're ready."

"I guess so. Got a few more places to go. Luckily on Saturday's I have a short day."

CHAPTER THIRTEEN

"That sister of yours is not going to make this easy on us is she." Rose said looking at Derek. Derek and Megan had actually been at Kat's house when Rose had called her. They had stripped all the beds and were doing an inventory on what all Kat had. Once Rose and Kat left, Derek and Megan were going to go shopping. Kat had just went shopping but Derek knew how his brother's appetite was. He was bringing three of his friends with him and if their appetites were the same, Kat was going to need a lot more food.

"Well of course she's not!" Derek said with a grin. "If she knew what we were up to she would really be giving us hell!"

"Wouldn't expect anything else from her!" Rose said smiling.

Megan came into the living room where Derek and Rose stood "I think we only have one load to wash and then all the beds will be done. How's everything else going?"

"I'm thinking we better not do a lot of lolly-gagging around. Otherwise, Kat will be on her way home and we may get caught." Rose said.

"Kat sure does have a beautiful place." Megan said looking around. "It's so peaceful here and I have always liked the log cabin look. No neighbors around; really nice"

"She has a pond back behind the house. I don't know if she still does a lot of fishing or not but she used to be on the dock or in her little John boat a lot." Derek said.

"She used to have a big get together every year, but she hasn't had one for a couple of years." Rose said.

"Probably because you went skinny dipping in her pond." Derek said grinning.

"What was I supposed to do? I didn't have a swim suit!" Rose protested.

Megan looked between the two. "Wait a minute, you two are actually serious! Miss Rose you actually went skinny dipping!"

"Well of course I did! It was hot and the pond looked too inviting."

"Of course, it didn't have anything to do with the amount you had to drink that night." Derek teased.

"Don't be stupid boy! I would have done it with just coffee in my system! "Rose snorted. "Ok, chop-chop kiddos, we need to get busy."

CHAPTER FOURTEEN

Kat was sitting at the bar talking to Leon and a few customers that had wondered in. It always amazed her that people could come into a bar before noon and start drinking. Of course, her own grandma started drinking vodka first thing in the morning. Her phone started ringing, interrupting her thoughts. She looked down to see that her grandma was calling her.

"Kathryn, we are heading your way." Her grandma said. "We have to stop so Derek can wash his jeep first but I think that is the only place we got to go."

"Ok. I'm just chillin' out here. Whenever you get here is fine." Kat told her.

Derek looked over at his grandma when she hung up her phone. "Why am I washing my jeep? It's not dirty."

"Kat is not going to believe we went muddin if your jeep is not clean. She knows how well you take care of it. If you went mudding the first thing you would do is wash it. If she sees your jeep and it does not look like it was just washed, she might be suspicious." Rose explained.

"Good thinking Miss Rose!" Megan said.

"Ok, let me get this straight. You are going to keep Kat away for as long as you can. Once Blake and his buddies show up, I am supposed to text you or call so you know it is ok for her to come home. Am I missing anything?" Derek asked.

"Nope, I think you got it. I just hope she doesn't suspect anything." Rose responded.

Within the hour Rose, Derek and Megan were pulling into Grumpy's Palace. They had talked to Blake on their way into town and he had told them that he wouldn't be there for another 5-6 hours.

Kat smiled at the three as they walked in. "I was getting ready to go home and take a nap!" Kat said. It had done her good to sit and just visit. A nap had sounded good though she thought with a sigh.

"You're too young to be taking naps during the day Kathryn! If you had listened to me and drunk your "special" orange juice you would be full of piss and vinegar!" her grandma said.

Derek smiled at his twin. "You know if you had a sex life you would maybe have a reason to be tired and take a nap" he teased.

Kat rolled her eyes "You just worry about your own sex life and I will worry about my lack of one!"

"You know Kat when I was your age me and your Grandpa used to bump uglies all the time! Wouldn't matter how tired we were, once he started touching my breasts…"

"Grandma!" Kat hollered. At the same time Derek said "Oh geez! Don't start talking like that or I am gonna throw up!"

Megan and Leon were both cracking up. "Never a dull moment with you around Miss Rose!" Leon said.

"You all are just a bunch of prudes!" Rose grumbled. "If you all would listen to me you might learn a thing or two. Megan if you want some advice on how to please your man you just come and visit me and we will have a chat. Kat, you don't have a man but when you do get one, we can have the same talk!"

Megan's face was beet red. "Umm, thank you Miss Rose. I will have to stop by sometime." She said laughing.

Derek looked over at Megan, "Just don't tell me if you do something to me that she has told you to try unless your wanting to kill the mood!"

"Well, ok then. Let's get going now Grandma. I think Megan has had enough for one day." Kat said getting up.

"Ok Kat. Where do you plan on going? Terra Haute or Champaign?" Rose asked.

"I think Terra Haute. I know my way around there better." Kat said not noticing the look that her Grandma and Derek exchanged.

"Well, let's get going. Maybe we can find you a man while we are out and about Kathryn." Rose said with a twinkle in her eye.

"We are going to go shopping for party stuff, not for me a man!" Kat said. "If I was going shopping for a man I sure the hell wouldn't have any of you all with me!"

"Why not sis? We would just have your best interest at heart you know." Derek said grinning.

"Oh, good grief! You all need to quit worrying about my love life. I'm leaving now Grandma. We've been yacking for too long. Daylight is wasting!" Kat said shaking her head.

"See you all later. Be careful on the road Kat." Leon said.

As Kat and Rose walked out the door Derek looked at Leon and Megan. "Well we've stalled as long as we can. It's up to Grandma to keep her away long enough for Blake to show up.

You ready to go shopping?" He said looking at Megan.

"Always!" Megan said grinning.

CHAPTER FIFTEEN

Sure, enough when they had walked outside Kat had looked at her brother's jeep and laughed. "Nice and shiny as always. I would have been surprised if he had come straight here without washing it" she told her grandma. Rose had just smiled and winked at her granddaughter.

They had been on the road for almost 45 minutes chatting about everything under the sun when Rose looked over at Kat and said "So, what all do you still have to get?"

"Well, there are a few things I want to check on. There are going to be pics of them all over the place; hanging from the ceiling, on the tables and I need to get some more poster board to set up as well. That I will probably just grab from Wal-Mart. I have vases and artificial flowers. The local flower shop is going to deliver some fresh flowers as well. I just need some additional decorations. To tell you the truth, I'm not sure exactly what I'm looking for; I will know when I see it though." Kat said getting off the Interstate.

"You have all the stuff for the food-plates, napkins, silverware? I know you said you ordered the food but what about the important stuff like the cake and ice cream?"

"The cake was one of the first things I got ordered. I figured I would just go to the store and get some gallons of ice cream the day of the party." Kat said pulling into the parking lot.

The store was huge and the parking lot was full when they pulled into the party store. "Grandma, let me know if you get tired of walking." Kat said.

"Oh, don't worry about me none. I'm going to latch on to one of the electric old people carts!" Rose said.

Kat grinned, "Try not to run over anyone" she told her.

They walked into the store and Rose grabbed the only electric cart that was there. She sat down on the electric cart and fiddled with all the buttons. "Well, it seems simple enough. Does it have a horn?"

Kat went on over to her grandma and examined the cart, "Doesn't look like there is one on it." She said.

"Well then I can't promise I'm not going to run over anyone if I don't have a horn to honk. I guess if they don't hear or see me coming then that's their fault." Rose said.

Kat shook her head, "Let's go see what we can find." She said walking to the side of the cart careful not to get in front of her grandma.

They wondered around the store for a while. Kat saying excuse me and apologizing several times when her grandma would almost run into people. "Kathryn they sure do have an assortment here, don't they," Rose said.

"Yes, they do. I would never have thought there would be this much stuff in a party store."

Rose stood up and got off the electric cart. "I need to stretch for a bit. That cushion could be a lot softer!"

While Rose and Kat were looking at an assortment of table decorations, a lady came up to the electric cart and started looking it over. Rose looked at the woman, "Is there something I can help you with?"

"Well, I was looking to see if it had a full charge or not. I hate it when people leave them in the aisle like this. There weren't any more carts up front when I got here." The lady said.

"I sure the hell hope you don't plan on sitting your ass on that one! I've been using it." Rose said.

The lady looked at Rose, "I don't see you on it; you must not need it too bad. I have two bad knees and I believe I need it more than you do" she said glaring at Rose.

"Oh crap!" Kathryn muttered.

"Well, let me tell ya, I do feel sorry for your knees carrying you around all the time. I think if you exercised a little bit more and lost some weight, they would probably be pretty grateful to you!" Rose said.

"What are you trying to say-that I'm fat!" the woman said raising her voice.

"If the pants fit. Of course, in your case they would have to be stretchy pants to fit. Do they make non-stretchy pants in your size?" Rose said with an angelic look on her face.

"Well I never!" the lady stormed.

"Well apparently you have otherwise you wouldn't be in the shape you're in." Rose countered.

"Is there a problem here?" said a voice from behind the ladies.

"This ole hag called me fat!" the lady hollered pointing her finger at Rose. She was getting so mad her face was turning red.

"Settle down there tubby! You're gonna give yourself a heart attack!" Rose said. "If you fall on the floor I sure the hell can't help you up!" Rose turned toward the store employee that was standing there just staring at the two women in bewilderment. "I never called her fat. I just told her to exercise and lose some weight and that would make her knees happy. It's not like her own doctor isn't telling her the same thing." Rose said matter-of-factly.

"Are you still using the cart ma'am?" the employee asked.

"As a matter-of-fact I am!" Rose said. "My butt would still be on it if it had some cushion on it. My butt started hurting so I had to stand up."

The employee looked at the other woman, "I'm sorry ma'am, this lady had the electric cart first so you will need to get a different one."

"I want to speak to the manager! This is ridiculous! She obviously doesn't need the cart otherwise she would still be on it. I wouldn't be in this situation if this store had an adequate number of carts in the first place! If she is going to keep this cart then I demand you bring me one here. I am not going to walk back up to the front of the store only to find out there are still none up there!" the lady stormed.

"I apologize for the inconvenience ma'am. I will get you a manager to come and talk to you. I will also send a request to the rest of our employees to see if we can find you a cart. Would you like for me to get you a chair so you can sit down while we find you a cart?"

"Better get her two chairs." Rose chimed in. "I'm not so sure one will hold her!"

Kat grabbed her grandma's arm, "Please just get back on

your cart so we can finish our shopping. Try not to let any more of your opinions leak out, this situation is getting out of hand."

"Excuse me, I'm going to grab the cart so we can finish our shopping." Kat said attempting to get the cart. The angry lady was still griping at the employee and had her hand on the handle of the cart.

"You really need to learn that old lady some manners!" the angry woman said to Kat.

Kat looked at the much larger woman, "I believe she is not the only one that could use some manners. You could use some too. My Grandma had this cart first, as soon as she told you that she was not done with it you should have done the grown-up thing and walked away. Instead you are standing here throwing a temper tantrum and growling at this poor employee who probably would have looked for an electric cart for you if you had just asked! You should be ashamed of yourself acting like this!"

"Is there a problem here?" a young man asked. He had come up from behind Kat and was smiling at the ladies.

"My Grandma and I were just leaving to finish our shopping." Kat exclaimed.

"You should have more electric carts in this store and have a policy that says only people who actually need to use them can ride on them!" the angry lady said.

"Well if that policy goes into effect, I will be able to still ride on one whereas if they put a weight limit on the carts you wouldn't be able to ride on any of them!" Rose said.

"Ladies, let's just calm down." He looked over at Kat, "I'm

the store manager. I'm sorry that you are having to go through this. Please have them call me up front when you get ready to check out. For your inconvenience I would like to give you a percentage off of your total purchase." He said flashing her a dazzling smile.

"That's not really necessary." She said smiling back at him.

"Now Kathryn, that would be rude of you to turn this young good-looking man down. We will have them holler at you when we get ready to check-out," Rose reassured him.

"Why do they get a discount? After that ole coot talked to me the way she did! If anyone deserves a discount it should be me!" the lady spluttered. "I guess if I was a young good-looking lady, I would be getting a discount as well!"

"If you were a young good-looking lady you wouldn't have a big ass and bad knees and we wouldn't be having this conversation!" Rose snapped.

The young manager looked like he was trying to hold in a laugh. "Actually, ma'am I wanted to apologize to you as well. I just apologized to them first since they were going to go ahead and finish their shopping. I fully intend on giving you a discount too." He said soothingly. "In fact, your own electric cart is coming down the aisle so you can rest your knees."

Kat took the opportunity of the lady being distracted to get her grandma and her cart away from the scene.

"Kathryn, are you sure we can't stay here? I would like to see if the tires go flat or how much of Tubby's butt is going to hang off the seat." Rose said.

"Absolutely not! We are going to get away from this lady before you make her stroke out!" Kat said.

They moved away from the scene with Rose muttering something about Kat not letting her have any fun and the cart needing a horn.

71

CHAPTER SIXTEEN

Kat picked up a few additional items for the party and found a few items for the club as well. She was beginning to think that the one special item that she was looking for was not going to be found when they started down a different aisle.

"Oh, that is it!" she gasped. The aisle she had just went down had a variety of candle holders. "I can put these on the tables. We wouldn't have that glaring light any more. Instead we could have a softer light that would soften the mood for everyone. Who doesn't like candlelight?" Kat said.

"You really think that will be a good idea Kathryn? A lot of the people that will be there will be drinking. I don't think drunkards need to be around fire!"

"Your right Grandma." She said her enthusiasm dying. "Wait a minute! What if we use the candles that take batteries? They flicker like real candles. If a drunkard knocks one over it won't catch the club on fire."

"Now that is a wonderful idea!" Rose said.

Kat smiled at her grandma. "With all that we have here, my shopping for the party supplies will be all done!"

She picked out a glass candle holder that looked like a flower. The leaves were green and were pointing upward, the stem curved up in a slight 'S' shape and the flower was a magenta color and looked like a rose. The candle would fit inside the flower. She sighed when they only had 20 on the shelf.

"I would like to have more of these," she exclaimed.

"Well, why don't you pick out a different one and then alternate them?" Rose asked.

"That will work, let's see if we can find something else that will look good next to it." Kat said looking at the large assortment around them.

After several minutes of holding other candle holders next to the ones that she had already picked out, Kat decided on a candle holder in the shape of a hummingbird. The candle would sit on the hummingbird's back.

"Mom loves hummingbirds and I think that they will look adorable together on the tables." Kat said pleased with her decision.

"I agree with you; your parents will appreciate your hard work Katherine." Rose said smiling softly at her granddaughter. "Now let's go holler for that good-looking man that is going to give you a discount. Maybe he will give you his phone number too. I did not see a wedding ring you know."

"Grandma! Stop trying to get me hooked up!" Kat said.

"Well someone has to help you. You're not doing a very good job on your own." Rose said.

CHAPTER SEVENTEEN

The two ladies made their way to the check-out with Rose telling Kat all the reasons why she should let her pick her out a man.

Kat started putting her items up on the check-out counter. Rose started talking to the young check-out girl as soon as they got up there, telling her to get the good-looking manager up there.

The young girl smiled at Rose and then paged the manager, "Josh to register 9 for customer service please."

Kat looked at her grandma and shook her head. "I told you that we were not going to bother him. It probably won't be that much of a discount anyway."

"Every little bit helps." Rose told her. Rose then turned to the check-out girl, "So Josh is his name? Well that fits him. Is Josh married or have a girlfriend?"

"Oh, good grief!" Kat said.

"To tell you the truth ma'am, I'm not sure. I know he is not married but I don't know if he has a girlfriend." The girl said.

"As a matter-of-fact he does not have a girlfriend," said Josh coming up behind them.

"Oh, good Lord!" Kat exclaimed her face flaming red. "I am really sorry! My grandma should have just kept her mouth shut; she doesn't get out much," said Kat glaring at Rose.

Josh just laughed. "She is fine. I feel kind of flattered that she was asking about me," he said smiling.

"Well, my granddaughter just happens to be single too. I think you two would make beautiful babies together!" Rose said.

Kat was hoping that a hole would open up and just take her somewhere other than where she was at.

"Well, if I am single and she is single, maybe we should meet sometime for dinner," Josh said smiling at Kat.

"That sounds like a fantastic idea!" Rose said clapping her hands together and smiling, clearly proud of herself.

"Well, sure. I guess we could have dinner sometime." Kat said wondering how all of this had just happened.

"I would like to know your name though, before we have dinner," he said.

"Of course. My name is Katheryn but everyone calls me Kat." She said smiling.

"Nice to meet you Kat," Josh said smiling at her.

Kat felt herself smiling back at him, "It is nice to meet you too. You really do not have to give us a percentage off."

"I know I do not have to, but from what my employee has told me, you deserve one. I got there just in time to hear you defend him. We really appreciate that." Josh said looking serious.

"You can apply the discount now, I have her purchase totaled up," the young check-out girl said.

"Let's see, your total is $451.92, with the discount your total will be $316.34," Josh said after hitting a few buttons.

"That's what 30% off? I was not expecting that much," Kat said, her eyes widening in shock.

"Now Katherine, thank the young good-looking gentleman." Rose scolded her.

"Thank you, Josh," said Kat, "that is very generous of you. I am stunned that the discount was that much." She looked over at her grandma who was watching the two young people with a big pleased look on her face.

Kat got her pocket book out of her purse and paid for the items. She looked around while she was waiting on her change, the store was not as crowded as it was when they first got there. The girl handed her change to her and gave her a big grin.

"Have a good day," the girl said and then looked back and forth between Kat and Josh.

"Are you ready to get something to eat and then head back home?" she asked her grandma.

Rose looked at her in astonishment, "Well, you need to give Josh your phone number first."

"You don't have to if you don't want to. You don't know me so I would completely understand." Josh said.

"Oh no, I will give you my number. I must warn you though, I am a pretty busy woman." Kat said somewhat flustered.

"I can understand that, I'm pretty busy myself. I tell you what, I will take your number and send you a text so you will have mine. Whenever you get time, shoot me a text and we will go from there."

"That sounds like a plan." She quickly jotted her phone number down on a piece of paper that he handed her and smiled as she handed the paper back to him.

She smiled and waved at him awkwardly before she started grabbing her sacks.

"Kat, can you get those bags alright? You have this strapping young man here to help you." Rose said.

Josh hurried over to her and started grabbing the bags, "If you don't mind, since you have a lot of stuff and some of it is breakable, why don't we put your bags in a cart and take the cart to your vehicle?"

Kat shook her head in agreement and started putting her bags in the cart. She was glad he had thought about putting it all in the cart. She should have thought about it herself; there is no way she would have been able to carry all the bags.

We can get this stuff out to my vehicle. Don't let my grandma push you around," Kat warned, "you let her get away with it and she will never stop. She is relentless!"

Josh started laughing as he started pushing the cart outside. "I will keep that in mind for future reference. Ok ladies, lead the way."

Kat walked ahead of Rose and Josh so she could open the trunk. She could hear them talking but could not make out the words they were saying. Part of her was not so sure she wanted to hear what her grandma was saying to him.

She opened the trunk of her mustang and then stepped back so they could get the cart up closer.

Josh whistled, "Sweet ride, this baby is yours?"

"Sure is," Kat said smiling proudly. She had wanted a mustang for a long time. When she had seen the beautiful blue car at the car dealership in town, she had stopped in on impulse. A test drive later and a call to the bank and Kat had her a new mustang.

"We can just get put the bags in here. I think they will be alright. I have a thick blanket back here in case of emergencies that we can wrap around the glass to cushion it." Kat said as she started opening up the blanket.

When Josh bent over to get the bags that were on the bottom of the cart, Kat just shook her head when she saw her grandma checking him out. When Rose noticed Kat watching her, she just smiled and gave her a thumb up.

Josh finished putting in the bags and shut the trunk. "Well, you two ladies have a safe trip home," he looked at Kat, "I hope I hear from you soon."

"Oh, you will," Rose chimed in.

Josh turned around after giving them both a heart stopping smile before taking the cart and heading back to the store.

When Kat and Rose got in the car, Kat turned to Rose. "Are you happy with yourself? You totally embarrassed me in there."

"Of course, I'm proud of myself. You just gave a good-looking man your phone number. That would not have happened if I hadn't been with you."

"Knowing my luck, he is some kind of psycho," Kat said. "Maybe he is like Charlie and all he wants to do is take me out to dinner, get me drunk and take advantage of me," she said grinning at her grandma.

Her grandma scowled at her, "You are just a regular comedian aren't you."

"Runs in the family," Kat said grinning.

CHAPTER EIGHTEEN

They decided to stop at a local steakhouse for a late lunch/ early supper.

"My mouth is watering just thinking about the steak I'm going to order." Rose said.

"Their steaks are good," Kat agreed, "but I am going to have that chicken dish. I don't remember what it is called but it has pasta, mushrooms, cheese, onion and bacon in it."

She pulled into the parking lot happy to find a parking spot up close. The restaurant was definitely not as crowded as it would be in a couple of hours.

"Only you would go to a steakhouse and order chicken." Rose smirked.

They walked into the restaurant and was greeted by a smiling hostess. "Just the two of you today?" she asked.

"Yes." Kat said before Rose could smart something off.

"Follow me please," the hostess said leading them to a corner booth. "Your server will be right with you."

Kat looked around her, taking in all of the items on the walls. One wall had autographed pictures of several musicians; there were even a few autographed guitars. Another wall had antique items such as farm tools, knick-knacks, old pictures and toys. On the other side of the restaurant they had a wall that was filled with nothing but pictures of kids and babies with funny sayings on them. In the center of the restaurant a bar in the shape of a circle was the focus. The wood gleamed and the chrome sparkled, it had obviously been taken good care of. There was just too much to take in.

A young man walked up to their booth, Introduced himself as Matt and asked them what they wanted to drink and if they would like to order an appetizer to start out with. Both ladies ordered a sweet tea and declined an appetizer.

"Well Kat, here's another young good-looking man serving us today. You play your cards right and he could be giving you his phone number too." Rose said winking at her granddaughter.

Kat groaned, "Do not embarrass me anymore than you already have today. Trying to hook me up with every young man we come into contact with is a little extreme isn't it?"

"Well of course not dear. You need to keep your options open; get you a few stallions to ride for a while. Besides you don't want a boyfriend, just someone to relieve some stress by giving you some sexual release at times." Rose said matter-of-factly.

"Oh, good Lord, you did not just say that!" Kat put her head in her hands, letting her golden hair fall across her face. "I am going to go to the bathroom. Do not cause any trouble while I'm gone." Kat warned.

When Kat left the restroom, Matt was at their table with their drinks talking to Rose. He had brought homemade bread with butter as well. Kat gave Rose a warning glare to which Rose smiled and winked at.

"I was just telling Matt how much you love this steakhouse. You two have a lot in common Kathryn! His favorite here is that chicken stuff you said you like. He also likes dogs and fishing. Isn't that something!"

"Yeah, that's something alright." Kat muttered.

"Are you ladies ready to order?" Matt asked them.

"Sure. I want the 8 oz steak, cooked well-done, a baked potato with butter and sour cream and a side salad with ranch dressing." Rose said.

"And you would like the "chicken stuff", he said smiling at Kat.

"Yes please. I would like the rice pilaf and green beans with that if you don't mind." Kat said.

"Good choice ma'am. Is there anything else I can get you ladies?" he asked looking at Kat.

"How about your phone number, young man?" Rose said grinning.

"Grandma! You are unbelievable. This young man is probably in a relationship. You can't just ask every Tom, Dick and Harry that we run into for their phone number."

"Well, of course I can. Besides I already asked him if he was single and told him that you are single too. I also told him that you didn't want a relationship, you just needed laid every now and then." Rose said, obviously proud of herself.

Kat stared at her grandma in horror, "You did not tell him that! What the hell is wrong with you?"

Rose looked over at Matt, "See, what did I tell you, she definitely needs laid."

"I am so sorry." Kat said her face flaming "I do not know

why she is behaving this way."

Matt smiled, "That's ok. I'm not offended or anything. In fact," he said looking into Kat's eyes, "if you want my phone number, I would be more than happy to give it to you."

Kat closed her eyes. This was turning into a nightmare.

"I'm sorry," Kat said again. "She shouldn't be asking personal questions like that."

"It is fine. I will get your orders turned in and will be back with them as soon as they are done." Matt said and then turned around and walked away.

Kat waited until he left before glaring at her grandma, "I am not going to take you anywhere if you can't behave. You try to get me a date one more time and I am leaving your crazy ole ass here." She hissed at her.

"Ok Kat. I would tell you I'm sorry but I would be lying. I will not try to set you up anymore tonight." Rose promised.

Kat sighed, "I guess that is the best I'm going to get from you."

CHAPTER NINETEEN

Matt came back several times to check on them before bringing their meal out. When he did bring their food out to them, he was accompanied by two other young men who kept glancing over at Kat. One of the guys was bold enough to keep invading Kat's space. At one point he was right up against her. Kat moved her body away from him, only to have him invade her space yet again.

Kat pretended not to notice their glances and would murmur a thank you to them occasionally. For once Rose did not make any comments as the young men placed their plates in front of them. After all their food was served, all three of the young men hovered around their booth.

Rose glanced up at them, "Are you boys waiting on a tip or what? If so, you're going to have to wait till we get done eating."

Rose turned her head to look at Kat. She could tell by the set of her shoulders that something was wrong.

"I do believe you boys have other customers waiting on your services." She looked over at Matt, "Would you be so kind as to get this caveman," she said pointing to the man that was crowding Kat, "away from my granddaughter before his drool lands in her food?"

Matt turned and looked at the other two men, "Thank you for your help gentlemen. Let's leave these two lovely ladies alone so they can enjoy their meal." He glanced back at the two women, "I apologize ladies. We will leave you to your food.

Please let us know if you need anything else," he said smiling and then left with the other two men.

A few minutes later, the guy who had been crowding Kat came back to their booth. He smiled at Kat and laid a folded piece of paper by her plate. With a big smile on his face he winked at her and went back towards the kitchen.

With a puzzled look on her face, Kat picked up the folded piece of paper, unfolded it and started reading. After reading the note she looked up at her grandma, her cheeks flushed.

"Well, what does it say?" Rose asked.

"He says that if I want to get laid to give him a call because he can rock my world. I hope your happy now. This Matt kid probably went and told all the guys that work here that I don't want a relationship; I just want to get laid!" She said as she stabbed angrily at her food.

"I'm sorry Kat. I didn't mean to have them guys come over here and act like idiots. That big oaf that was standing by you was making you uncomfortable. I regret the words that came out of my mouth. I should never have told Matt that you needed laid," her grandma put her fork down. "In fact, I'm going to set this straight." Rose wiped her mouth off and stood up.

"What are you doing?" Kat asked looking at her grandmother suspiciously.

"I told you, I'm going to set things straight!" Rose said as she started walking toward the kitchen.

"Oh crap!" Kat said as she watched her grandmother walk away. "I better eat what I can now before she gets us kicked out of here."

Kat went back to eating, occasionally glancing up trying to catch a glimpse of Rose. She would catch a glimpse of her small frame only to lose her when she went behind one of the tall booths. At one point she did catch sight of her talking to Matt, only to have both of them disappear into the kitchen.

Kat had been around her grandmother all her life and had witnessed her doing some off the wall things. Truthfully it wouldn't have surprised her any if her grandma had come out of the kitchen riding a unicycle with a clown nose on.

When her grandmother did finally make her way out of the kitchen, she thankfully didn't have a clown nose and was not riding a unicycle. She sat back down and started eating her food as if she hadn't just come back from the restaurant's kitchen.

"So, how long do I have to finish eating before they come to throw us out?" Kat asked between bites.

"I didn't do anything to get us thrown out of here yet." Rose said keeping her eyes on her food.

Kat looked up to see Matt heading back to their table with one of the guys who had been with him earlier when he had served them food. Kat was glad to see that it was not the same one that had gave her the note.

"What did you do now?" Kat said looking at her grandmother.

Rose just smiled slightly and kept eating.

Matt and the other young man stopped at their table. Matt cleared his throat and looked at Kat.

"I wanted to apologize for our behavior. I should never have repeated what your Grandma said to me. I did not know that Pete was going to do what he did."

"I apologize as well ma'am. My name is Ed and my momma did not raise me to act like that," the other young man said.

"Where is the creeper at, the guy named Pete?" Rose asked.

Matt hesitated, "He said he didn't have anything to apologize for and if you were going to tell strangers that your granddaughter needed laid, then that was probably the case and he would be doing her a favor. He said he was just gonna try to give her additional customer service."

"He said what!" Rose spluttered.

Kat just looked at the two young men. Her face showing a shocked look.

"Oh, that's it! Someone needs to teach this punk a lesson." Rose got back up and stalked back towards the kitchen.

"Would one of you guys go in there and have her come back out here? He is not worth the trouble and I have lost my appetite."

A loud commotion from the kitchen made everyone in the restaurant stop what they were doing.

A male voice hollered "Are you crazy lady; you can't be hitting people with my big pan!"

"Watch me! This little jackass owes my granddaughter an apology and we are not leaving until she gets one."

Another loud bang and Rose came stalking back out of the kitchen holding Pete by the ear and heading towards their booth.

A lady dressed in professional clothes, wearing a name badge that said Manager, came hurrying towards Rose.

"What is the meaning of this? You need to let go of his ear immediately!"

"Buzz off, this jerk owes my granddaughter an apology."

"She's freaking crazy, June. Ger her the hell away from me. Ouch!" he yelled as Rose jerked on his ear harder.

"Now apologize to her." Rose commanded.

"Ok, ok, I'm sorry!" he sputtered.

Rose let go of his ear. As soon as she let go, Pete raised his fist up.

CHAPTER TWENTY

Fearing that he was getting ready to hit her grandmother, Kat grabbed her plate and smacked Pete upside the head with it. Her food went all over the place.

Total chaos erupted.

Pete fell to his knees, the Manager tried getting in-between Pete and the ladies and Rose stood up on the booth seat and started hollering obscenities at Pete and the Manager.

Matt, eyes wide, was trying to get everyone calmed down.

Kat watched the plate fall to the floor. Had she really just smacked Pete upside the head with her plate? Maybe she was more like her grandmother than she wanted to admit.

She went over to Rose and proceeded to try to get her down. Once she had succeeded in getting Rose down from the booth seat, she started gathering their things.

"Come on, help me get our stuff gathered up so we can get out of here." Kat said.

"I'm not even done with my dinner. I say let's just sit back down and eat. I will share my steak with you. That is the least I can do after you went all Babe Ruth on that punk."

"I don't think you two ladies are going to go anywhere until the cops show up," the Manager told them. She had helped Pete to one of the near-by chairs to sit down. She was standing with her hands on her hips, looking at the mess that had been made. Pete was wearing most of what was not on the floor, but she had some noodles stuck to her slacks. The white noodles were very noticeable against the black slacks.

"You might want to get that dickweed employee of yours some napkins or a wash cloth. He has food all over him." Rose said.

Matt came up to the Manager, "June, I think you better hear the whole story before you start jumping to conclusions."

"All I know is that this lady," she said pointing her finger at Rose, "had Pete by the ear and caused a scene in the kitchen and then this one," she said pointing to Kat, "hit him with her food plate."

"Well, if your employee had acted like an employee should, instead of a cocky, jiggalo-wanna-be, we wouldn't be having this conversation." Rose said.

Kat picked up the note that was on the table and handed it to the Manager.

"Maybe you should read what your employee left me."

June looked down at the note and then looked from Matt to Pete.

"Would one of you like to explain this to me? Actually, why don't we all go to my office so we can continue this conversation." June raised her voice so the rest of the restaurant could hear her.

"I apologize to everyone for what just happened. Please enjoy a dessert or an appetizer on the house."

A murmur went through the small crowd that was in the restaurant as June ushered Rose, Kat, Matt and Pete toward a hallway that went past the kitchen.

Rose was attempting to juggle her drink, salad bowl and plate as she followed June to her office.

"Would you like for me to help you with that ma'am?" Matt asked her.

"That would be wonderful, thank you." Rose said as he took her plate and salad bowl from her.

June stood at the door as everyone entered. There were only two chairs in the room in front of June's desk and both of the ladies went to sit down. Pete attempted to sit in one of them but when Rose threatened to throw her tea on him, he went and stood by the door after June shut it.

After helping Rose get situated, Matt went and stood against the wall.

"Matt, can you go get an ice pack for his eye?" June asked as she took her seat.

"Sure, be right back," Matt said.

June looked through the papers on her desk, not saying a word to anyone. Rose continued to eat her food and Kat just looked around the office. Once Matt got back with Pete's ice pack, June looked up at the four people in her office. She made a steeple with her fingers and let out a loud sigh.

"I imagine that this is going to be quite the story. Who wants to begin?"

Rose took another drink of her tea. "Well, I might as well start. I guess the short version is that I was trying to get my granddaughter hooked up with this charming boy," Rose said pointing at Matt, "I could have used different words when talking to him. I umm told Matt that she needed laid but didn't want a relationship. I'm assuming that he went and told some of his buddies what I said which is why this idiot left the note for Kat."

June looked over at Matt, "Is this true Matthew?"

Matt moved restlessly against the wall, "For the most part. I went to the kitchen after talking to them and I guess I had a big smile on my face because Justin asked me why I looked like the cat that swallowed the canary. Pete was standing by us so he heard everything I told Justin. I didn't know the big dummy was going to do something stupid like bring her a note."

June looked at Pete who kept his eyes on the floor in front of him.

"What do you have to say for yourself?"

"I don't have anything to say. Matt told us that the old lady told him that her granddaughter needed laid. I was just trying to provide excellent customer service," he said with a smirk.

"Are you serious? What would make you think that giving one of our guests a note like that would be acceptable?" June sighed and, looked at Rose, "Let me guess, this is when you went after Pete and dragged him out to apologize?"

"Nope. Matt and his buddy came up and apologized to Kat. Mr. Studpants over there decided he was not going to apologize to her cause he had not done anything wrong. That is when I went and grabbed him by the ear so he could apologize." Rose said barely glancing up as she put another bite of her steak in her mouth.

Kat sighed, "I am sorry this all escalated ma'am. My

Grandmother should not have said what she did. I shouldn't have smacked Pete upside the head but I thought he was going to hit my Grandma."

A knock sounded at the door, "June? There are a couple of policemen waiting to talk to you."

"Bring them on back here please Karen."

A moment later a middle age woman opened the door and escorted two policemen in.

"Thank you, Karen. Please make sure we are not interrupted."

"Yes ma'am," Karen said as she closed the door behind her.

"Thank you for showing up gentlemen. Things have calmed down a bit. At this time, I am not sure if any charges will be filed."

"Miss Rose, is that you? You're not causing any problems, are you?" one of the young officers said smiling at her.

"Tommy Jones, is that you? How's your momma doing? I haven't seen either one of you in a coons age." Rose said smiling at the young man.

"She's doing alright. She's still working at the Grocery Store downtown. This is my partner, Clark." Tommy said as he turned toward his partner. "Clark, this is Miss Rose and her granddaughter Kat. They are both from my hometown," he said motioning to the two women.

"Nice to meet you," Clark said nodding his head in the direction of the two ladies.

"If your momma is still working at the store, that would explain why Grandma hasn't seen her." Kat said laughing.

"You're not still banned from going in there are you, Miss Rose?" Tommy said, his eyebrows arching upward in surprise.

Rose shifted uncomfortably in her seat. "The last time I ran into Travis, the store owner, he told me I could come back in just as long as Carol wasn't in there," she snorted.

Tommy looked over at Clark, "I will have to tell you that story later. Remind me when we get back in the car, it's a good one."

Clark smiled, "I am sure it will be a good one."

"So, what's going on?" Tommy said looking over at June, his face suddenly getting serious.

"Well," June sighed.

"I might as well start," Rose grumbled, "I've been trying to get Kat a man and I kind of told Matt that she just needed laid, not really a relationship. Matt opened his mouth in the kitchen about what I said to him and then this idiot," she said pointing over to Pete, "gave her a note while she was eating telling her that if she wanted laid then he would take care of her. Actually, I think the words he used were "he could rock her world". Anyway, since I'm the one who opened my mouth, I said I was going to fix it. I went and told Matt what happened and asked him to apologize and have his buddies apologize as well. Numb nuts over there wouldn't apologize so I went and dragged him out of the kitchen by his ear. When I let go of his ear, he raised his hand like he was going to hit me and that is when Kat smacked him upside the head with her plate." Rose stopped so she could get a drink of her tea.

"Yeah, I guess that sums it up." June said.

The two cops were staring at the elderly lady in bewilderment.

"So, let me get this straight," Tommy started, "you told him," he said pointing at Matt, "that Kat needed laid but not a relationship. After you told him this, he went into the kitchen where he told his buddies what Miss Rose said."

"And then he," Clark continued pointing at Pete, "gave Kat a folded-up note saying he could "rock her world". Miss Rose then proceeded to the kitchen and dragged him out by the ear to get him to apologize to Kat."

"After he apologized to her," Tommy continued, "Miss Rose let go of his ear and Kat thought he was going to hit her grandma so she took her tray and hit him upside the head. Is this correct?"

"I would say you got it pretty well summed up." June said.

"Does everyone agree that this is what happened?" Tommy said.

Everyone nodded their heads but Pete.

Rose said, "Of course that is what happened. All you got to do is just look at this boy" she said pointing to Pete, "to know he doesn't play with a full deck."

"I take it you do not agree with this version?" Tommy said looking at Pete.

"I didn't mean anything by giving her the note. Her grandma is completely off her rocker but I wasn't going to hit her," he said defensively. He looked over at Kat and pointed his finger in her direction. "She had no right or reason to hit me with her tray. They both need locked up for battery," Pete snarled.

"You really want to try to press charges on an elderly lady, no offense Miss Rose, and Kat here who is a little bitty thing?"

Tommy said incredulously.

"Well, that is the stupidest thing I have ever heard. You try to press charges on us and you will be the laughing stock of the whole town. An old lady like me and a young woman like Kat got the best of a young dumb buck like yourself. Well, that is pathetic. I guess you can't fix stupid though." Miss Rose said.

"Then there is the publicity that may come about from all of this. This establishment will be known for the employee who sexually harassed a customer and then was smacked upside the head when he raised his hand to hit an elderly woman." Kat added.

Pete's face went through all kinds of different expressions, starting with anger and resentment before going to confusion and ending with resignation.

"No offense dude, but you would be screwed if you went through with this." Matt said.

June looked at Pete, "You have two options, one you apologize to these lovely ladies for being an ass and we all go on with our lives or two, you press charges on these ladies, who in turn will probably press charges on you and this all turns into quite the fiasco. I will probably have to fire you because you sexually harassed a customer. If the press gets wind of this, they will probably print a story with your picture included. This happens then everyone is going to know that two women got the best of you and that you got smacked upside the head by the woman that you sexually harassed because you raised your hand toward her Grandma. That is not mentioning all the bad publicity you will give this place."

"Come on boy, even you can't be that ignorant. In my opinion that is not a hard decision." Rose said staring at Pete when he just looked at June.

Pete took the ice pack off of his face. His face was already a little discolored but Kat was unsure if it was from the ice or from the impact of the tray. "If we all just forget this happened then I get to keep my job?" he asked.

"For now. You would be put-on probation and would have to work in the kitchen and have no contact with our customers for a while. I can't have one of my employees handing our customers inappropriate notes. If I even catch you looking at one of our customers wrong you will be out the door. Understand?" June asked, the look on her face giving no indication that she meant anything but business.

Pete nodded his head, "I understand ma'am. I won't let that happen again. I guess it would be for the best if we all just forgot this ever happened."

Rose looked at Pete, "If you have an inkling to "rock someone's world", you know they have women that will gladly let you do whatever you want to them for the right price," she said.

"I have never had to pay a woman for sex before. There are plenty of women out there who would probably pay me; I've never had any complaints." Pete said proudly.

"You actually think a woman would tell you that you were terrible in bed? Most women are not going to tell a man that. If anything, they will probably fake an orgasm just to get the guy off of them." Rose said.

Tommy shook his head and laughed at Miss Rose's words. "You haven't changed at all. If no one is going to file any charges then we are going to get out of here." He looked at

Miss Rose and Kat, "I hope you two are going back home. I don't need any more calls concerning you two. Kat, I will probably stop in at Grumpy's Palace next time I go see Mom. Miss Rose, I will tell Mom you said hello."

"Sure thing, Tommy. Hope to see you soon," Kat said.

"You make sure you do that." Miss Rose told him, "I will have to stop by the store sometime to see her; just as long as Carol is not there I'm allowed in there."

Tommy looked over at Pete, "I do not want to come back here with someone saying that you have been doing or saying inappropriate things to the customers. I will not be so nice next time," he looked over at Rose, "Miss Rose, please try to think about what you're saying before it comes out of your mouth."

Rose looked up at him sheepishly, "I will try to work on that."

"Glad to hear it. You all have a good evening," Tommy said as he and Clark headed out the door. Clark smiled and tipped his hat at them. Before the door shut, they all heard Clark ask his partner why Miss Rose was not allowed in a store and who Carol was.

June looked at the remaining people in her office, "I hope this has all been handled to everyone's satisfaction."

"Sure, no harm done, well except to his face but I don't see it hurting anything." Rose began.

"Thank you for handling this ma'am. My grandmother and I are going to be leaving now. I'm sorry for the ruckus that ensured with us here." Kat said. She looked over at Pete and Matt, "I am sorry that I hit you with the tray but I really did think that you were going to hit her," she said to Pete. "I'm sorry my Grandma told you all that stuff. She had no right saying that stuff to you." She added to Matt.

Matt smiled at Kat, "I know it may be wrong but I feel kind of honored that she was trying to hook me up with you. I am sorry for opening my mouth though."

June looked over at Pete, "Do you have something you would like to say?"

Pete looked over at her and rolled his eyes.

"That is your cue to apologize dummy," Rose said.

Pete gave her a dirty look, "I'm not stupid lady. I figured that out on my own."

"Well, I'll be, stupid can be taught!" Rose said in mock surprise.

"Grandma, behave." Kat warned

"I didn't actually mean to say stupid, I should have just called him a dummy." Rose smirked.

Pete gave the elder lady another dirty look and then turned to Kat, "I'm sorry I offended you with my note and I am shameless that you thought I was going to hit her."

"You didn't really mean to say shameless, did you? Don't use big words if you don't know their meaning. You probably meant regret, or at least I hope that you meant regret instead of shameless. Of course, you regret it, she whacked you upside the head with a tray!" Rose said grinning.

June stood up, "Ok guys, let's get back to work. Ladies, your meal is on the house. I hope you do not hold Pete's actions against us and I hope you come back again."

Pete did not waste any time in opening the door and leaving with ice pack in hand. Matt lingered a bit but after a look from June he smiled and walked out the door.

"Well, I hope you wouldn't charge Kat, all her food wound up on the floor or all over numbnuts." Rose said getting out of her seat.

"Are you sure you don't want us to pay for our food?" Kat asked dubiously, "I mean we did eat a big portion of it." Kat also rose from her seat.

"No, truthfully I would just like to see you ladies leave. I've had enough drama for one night." She followed the ladies out her door. Low enough that Rose could not hear her, June said "You sure do have your hands full with her."

Kat looked at her and nodded, "Thank you again. I appreciate your help with getting this all straightened out and again I am sorry for the chaos that erupted earlier."

"Would you mind if I get a sweet tea to go? Maybe some of the mints you leave on the ticket you all give us when we get to leave as well?" Rose asked.

June smiled at Rose, "Sure." She turned and looked at Kat, "Would you like one as well?"

"Actually, yes if you don't mind. A sweet tea sounds great."

"I don't mind at all." June said smiling, "Please wait right here and I will be right back."

As the woman was walking away, Rose turned and looked at her granddaughter, "Why do you reckon that she wants us to stay in this hall instead of out in the restaurant?"

"Seriously? We just caused a scene. I am sure she would like to get us out of here a soon as possible but doesn't trust us to be back in public." Kat said shaking her head. "I can't blame the poor woman one bit. It must have been some site for her to look over and see you dragging one of her employees out of the kitchen by the ear and then having me hit the same employee upside the head with my tray. I would probably be anxious to get us out of here too; can't blame her for keeping us back here."

Kat looked down at her watch, "Wow, I did not realize it was getting this late. It's been a long day and I am ready to go home and go to bed."

"Is it ok with you if I stay at your house another night? It is getting late and I will just wait to talk to Liz tomorrow." Rose said.

"That is fine. I can drop you off at your house tomorrow on my way to the club." Kat said yawning.

"Can we stop and get me some more Vodka for my orange juice on the way back to your place?" Rose asked.

"Do you need more orange juice too? As much Vodka as you use, orange juice probably lasts you quite a while."

"As a matter of fact, orange juice does last me quite some time. I always seem to run out of Vodka before my orange juice is gone. In fact, I usually go through 2-3 bottles of Vodka to one bottle of orange juice," Rose mused, "You know, I never really thought of that before. I think I need to write the Vodka company and tell them they need to start making their bottles bigger!"

Kat shook her head, "You know that does not surprise me

one bit. We can go through the gas station's drive thru and get you some Vodka before we head back to my house. Are you wanting to get in the hot tub tonight?"

"Sure, that sounds great. Do I have to…" Rose began.

"Wear clothes? Absolutely! I am thinking about getting in there and I do not want the picture of you naked in my head before I go to bed." Kat scolded her.

"Here are your sweet teas ladies. Here is also a small bag of mints for you to take home. Can I please ask you to quietly head to the door and not cause a scene?" June asked hopefully.

"Well it depends on if your employees behave themselves. I would hate to lay the smack down on someone for upsetting my granddaughter again!" Rose said.

"We will not cause a scene will we," Kat said giving her grandmother a warning look.

"No, I guess we will be quiet," Rose grumbled.

Kat quickly walked out into the restaurant and headed for the EXIT sign without making eye contact with anyone. Rose on the other hand, walked at a slow pace looking everyone in the eye while having a big smile on her face.

Most of the employees gave the ladies curious glances but none of them approached the two women.

Once Kat reached the door, she turned around expecting her Grandma to be right behind her but instead found her only half-way across the restaurant looking around smiling at everyone.

"Grandma, hurry up," Kat said.

Her grandma looked over at her, smiled wider and then put her finger up to her mouth and said 'Shhh'.

"Are you seriously "shushing" me? Unbelievable. Hurry up, everyone is going to think you are a simpleton with that big smile on your face."

"Well, Kat, we were asked to be quiet and to not cause a scene. I'm behaving myself and you're the one not being quiet." Rose said smugly as she finally reached the door.

"Let's just go home. I've had about enough excitement for the day." Kat said walking out into the parking lot. She didn't notice the small twitch of her grandmother's mouth as she walked behind her.

CHAPTER TWENTY-ONE

"You need me to stop again?" Kat asked, "You can't hold it until we get home?"

"I'm an old lady and my bladder is not what it used to be. Unless you want me to pee on your fancy smancy seats, I suggest you stop at the next place possible. If you don't, I'm not responsible for any of my accidents that might happen!"

Kat glanced over at her grandma, "Maybe I should buy you some Depends in case you have an accident. Oh wait, I know, I will get you some of those puppy pads to put on my seat."

"Oh, your funny. Just wait till you get my age. I hope you have a mouthy brat sitting next to you being disrespectful." Rose snapped. "Besides, you buy me some Depends and I am going to run around with a pair of them on my head and be bare assed hollering your name."

"You probably would too," Kat laughed. "We are less than 2 miles to the next exit. Can you wait that long?"

"Well, you better hope I can." Rose grumbled. She sat all the way back in the seat, crossed her legs and closed her eyes. "I had a good day today Katherine. We should do this more often."

Kat looked over at her grandma and noticed how tired she looked. "You feeling ok, grandma?"

"Sure honey, just been a long day."

"Yes, it has." Kat agreed. "You have been busy. You went

muddin with my brother, got into an argument with a lady over a mobile cart and then just about got arrested at a steak house. Most people don't have that much happen in a month let alone one day," Kat said as she turned her blinker on to get off the interstate.

"Don't forget I got you hooked up with the stud at the Party Store and almost had you another guy lined up if that creep hadn't messed everything up." Rose said opening her eyes and smiling at her granddaughter.

"I think I will go in with you to stretch my legs," Kat said as she pulled into a parking spot at the gas station.

"I don't care if you come in or not, I gotta go!" Rose said unbuckling her seatbelt and opening the door.

Kat laughed, for an elder lady her grandmother sure could move when she needed to, she thought to herself as she got out of her car.

She wandered around inside the gas station looking at all the trinkets. When Rose came out of the bathroom, she found Kat looking at a display of magnets.

"These are hilarious!" Kat said spinning the display.

"Honey, you really need to get out more often." Rose said.

"After getting out with you today I will not have to get out again for quite some time. I will be able to just go to work and go home to enjoy some peace and quiet; at least until Mom and Dad's party gets here."

"Or until Blake gets here," Rose laughed.

"That is for sure. He will not let me have any peace and quiet once he gets here. I don't know where he gets all of his energy. He wears me out just watching him," Kat said as she stifled a yawn.

"I'm ready to go if you are Kathryn. I'm surprised you haven't got yourself a snack or something; you didn't really eat a lot."

"I am starting to get a little snacky but I am going to wait until we get home."

"Oh crap, I got to get my Vodka!" Rose exclaimed. "Might as well get it here, this way we won't have to make any more stops," she said as she headed toward the cooler.

"Lord forbid we forget your Vodka," Kat retorted.

"Good Lord Kat, the prices here are outrageous," Rose said looking at the bottle she just got out of the cooler.

"If you don't want to get it here, I can stop in Effingham on our way home." Kat told her.

"Oh no," Rose said quickly, "I am going to go ahead and get it here." She shut the cooler and headed up to the check-out counter. "You should be ashamed of yourself charging people this much for a bottle of spirits," she said to the boy behind the counter, "This is highway robbery!"

"Lady, I just work here. I don't make the prices for this stuff. No one said you had to buy your booze here. You are more than welcome to go somewhere else," he said.

"Does your boss know you talk to your customers like that?" Rose said looking at the boy with disgust. "Does he know that you dress this way while you are at work?"

"What's wrong with the way I dress?" he said looking down at his clothes. His Pink Floyd t-shirt had a hole near the bottom and under one arm while there was a big red stain visible in the middle of the shirt. The blue jeans he was wearing had multiple rips in them.

"What's wrong with the way you're dressed? I've seen hoboes dressed better. Your shirt looks like a rag someone would use in a garage. The pants you are wearing either need patched or thrown in the garbage. I guess you could also put them in the garage where you got your shirt from," Rose said looking the boy up and down.

"I bought these jeans this way. I just grabbed the first shirt I saw because I was running late," the boy said looking at Rose in bewilderment.

"You spent money on jeans that already had holes in them? That doesn't make any sense. Someone seen you coming from a mile away. Was you wearing a shirt that said "I'm with stupid" while walking down the street by yourself?"

"Lady, I don't have a shirt that says "I'm with stupid," the boy said looking at Rose with confusion.

"Come on Grandma, let's just pay for your vodka and get going. The kid is right though, jeans with holes in them are a current fad." Kat said.

"I need a drink," Rose muttered. She paid for her vodka and then immediately opened the bottle and took a big drink.

"Geez lady, couldn't you have waited until you got home? Maybe you should check yourself into a rehab or something," the kid said as he watched in amazement as the elderly lady took another swig.

"Don't worry about me, I bought this fair and square. I'll go to rehab whenever you get a job as a fashion model," Rose said taking another swig. "Ok, let's go home Kat!"

Once in the car Kat looked over at Rose and shook her head, "After the way today has went, I am surprised you didn't try to hook me up with him," she said pointing back at the gas station.

"Don't be silly Kat. He was dressed like a bum and his cologne was stinky. You at least got to be with a guy who smells good. I don't want you to come over to my house with some guy who smells like the city dump."

Kat shook her head as she pulled back onto the interstate.

#

Derek laughed as he put his phone on the counter. He looked at the small group of people who were gathered in Kat's kitchen.

"Grandma says they will be here shortly. She doesn't think Kat will stop for her to "pee" anymore," he said making quote marks with his fingers in the air. "Kat has already told Grandma that she is going to buy her some Depends and put Puppy Pads on her seat."

The small grouped started laughing.

"I wish I was a fly on the wall around them two so I could listen and watch them." Blake said grinning.

Blake was leaning against Kat's counter. Derek was standing next to him with his arms around Megan. Liz, Allison, Grant and Leon all sat at the kitchen table along with 2 of Blake's friends, Reggie and Travis, who had already met Kat and Miss

Rose previously.

The last guy that Blake had brought with him was leaning against the counter on the other side of him. Shawn was the only one of the group who had never met Kat or Miss Rose. On occasion Blake was known to bring some of his workers home with him.

Blake looked over at Shawn with a grin on his face, "Reggie and Travis have already met Kat and Grandma, so they know what to expect but you my friend are in for a real treat."

Shawn smiled at Blake, "You have told me a lot of stories about your grandma, I must admit some of them have been kind of hard to believe but I am looking forward to meeting her."

"I can guarantee you that I didn't have to exaggerate on any of my stories when it comes to Grandma; she is one of a kind. None of us know what she is going to say or do next," Blake said. "Once you meet her all doubt will go away about whether or not I have been exaggerating."

The group all started laughing and agreeing with what Blake had said. They all had plenty of stories and memories regarding Rosy Davis.

"You are in for a treat when you meet Kat too. She can get pretty wound up."

"She gets more wound up around you Blake than she does with anyone." Derek said grinning at his brother.

"What can I say, I have that effect on people. Besides, I enjoy watching her when she gets irritated with me. She gets all fired up and you can just see the smoke coming out of her ears. It has been awhile since I have had a chance to annoy her," he said with a mischievous look in his eyes.

"There have been quite a few times where she has gotten you though," Derek said laughing. "Remember the time when you ticked her off when you put the dead fish in the bed of her pick-up? Remember what she did to get even with you?"

"How could I forget! She put a bunch of snakes in my truck." Blake shivered as he thought about the day he had opened his truck door ready to go to work and had seen around 10 snakes in the cab of his truck. Everyone knew that Blake did not like snakes at all.

"I will never forget that day, Blake paid me to come and get them out of his truck," Travis said laughing.

"No way in hell was I going to get them out of there. I would have bought me a new truck before I did that." Blake said shaking his head.

"I think I am more worried about meeting your sister than I am your grandma. I mean, we are at her house without her knowing it, getting ready to stay here uninvited." Shawn said.

"You don't have anything to worry about Shawn. Kats a great girl. She won' t hold this against you; this will all be on these two," Grant said pointing at the two brothers.

"All the ladies I have met when I have come home with Blake have been really sweet. Most of them have been real pretty too," Reggie said glancing over at Allison.

"Kat is a very pretty girl but we all know you were really talking about Allison," Travis said laughing.

"What am I, chopped liver!" Liz intervened.

"You know what I mean Liz. I think you are pretty too but you know that you are pretty. Kat is oblivious to how guys look at her," Travis said.

They all laughed at Travis's statement.

"You got me on that one," Liz said. "I tried to talk her into trying out for the Effingham County Fair Queen one year. She just shook her head at me and told me that I would win because I was beautiful and was made for stuff like that. I think if it had been a fishing tournament, she would have been one of the first ones to sign up," she said smiling as she thought fondly of her cousin.

"She has never been real girly," Derek agreed. "She has always been the kind that would rather be doing her own thing like fishing or reading a book rather than going shopping or having her nails done."

"Which is what makes Kat her own person. She's never been one to follow a crowd unless it was something she wanted to do. She is probably one of the most stubborn women I have ever known. On the other hand, she is also one of the most compassionate and caring person I know." Grant said.

"None of us would want Kat to be any other way," Allison agreed. "Of course, growing up with them two," she said gesturing toward Blake and Derek, "I don't think there is any way that she could have grown up girly," She teased.

Derek's phone started buzzing on the counter beside him. He glanced down at it and got a big grin on his face.

"It's Grandma. They are probably 5-10 minutes away. Showtime people!"

CHAPTER TWENTY-TWO

"I sure am glad to be home," Kat said as she pulled onto the lane that led her to her house.

"Me too, Kat. I am ready for bed. I think I will have a little drink before I lay down to help me relax," her Grandma said.

"No hot tub?" Kat asked smiling at her grandma. Her smile turned to a look of puzzlement, "Why didn't you leave any of the lights on in the house? You know I usually leave the light on above the stove. You didn't shut the garage door either."

"I guess I didn't think we would be gone all day," Rose responded. "You can blame your brother on the garage door. He was going to come back here and get your lantern out of the garage. He and Megan were going camping."

"I am going to beat him if there are any critters that have got in there; especially if a skunk got in. Oh well I'll go unlock the door and then get this stuff in the house. I think it will probably take a couple of trips. I don't want to trip and accidently break one. Why don't you go ahead and stay inside and rest?" Kat asked.

"Oh, heaven forbid if that was to happen. You would have to go back to that Party Store and see Josh," her grandma teased.

Kat got out of her car with her keys in hand. "That's odd, the door leading from the garage into the house isn't closed all the way. You did shut the door when you left didn't you?"

"I thought I did Kathryn, but I am an old lady who gets distracted easily."

"Surely Derek would have noticed the door and pulled it shut," Kat mused out loud.

"Well it is Derek you are talking about," Rose reminded her.

"But still…. better to be safe than sorry," Kat said softly as she picked up a whiffle ball bat.

"A whiffle ball bat? That's what you pick up to defend us," Rose whispered. "Besides, as loud as your car is, I don't think we snuck up on anyone."

Kat gave her a look and said, "It's not like I keep a gun in my garage!"

Kat slowly opened the screen door and pushed the main door open. Just as she stepped inside a shadowy figure came around the corner. Without thinking Kat swung the bat.

"Ow! What the hell!" a voice yelled.

"Blake? Is that you?" Kat turned the lights on to see her brother holding his nose.

"You trying to kill me or what?" Blake asked.

"With a whiffle ball bat? Seriously?" Kat said still a little bewildered that her brother was standing in her house.

"What I want to know," Rose said, "is how in the world did she manage to hit you in the nose; you're like the Jolly Green Giant next to Little Sprout."

"He was trying to be sneaky," Derek said. He had been laughing so hard that he was gasping trying to get the whole sentence out.

"Ok, funny, ha ha, now could someone please give me

medical attention?" Blake said.

"Well that is what you get for scaring the crap outta me," Kat snapped. "What in the world are you doing in my house? I thought you were not supposed to be here till later this week or next."

"Is this your way of saying "hi big brother, how you been? I sure have missed you." Blake asked her grumpily

"Well honey, you should be grateful that she didn't hit you with a food tray like she did to a guy earlier today," Rose said matter-of-factly, just as if she was talking about the weather.

"What?" said both brothers in unison.

"She thought the jerk was going to hit me so she swung her food tray at him." Rose said smiling obviously liking everyone's confusion. "I was so proud of her!"

Kat sighed, "Why don't we all go to the kitchen. I think we have a lot to talk about."

CHAPTER TWENTY-THREE

"It sure sounds like you two had quite the day. I'm glad I didn't have to make a trip all the way to Terra Haute to bail you both out of jail! So, Kat, when is your stud from the Party Store going to call you?" Derek asked his sister with a big grin.

They all were gathered in Kat's kitchen. A few folding chairs had been retrieved from the garage so that everyone who had wanted a seat had one. They all had a big laugh after hearing the stories of what had taken place while Kat and Miss Rose had been gone. At times the laughter had been so hard that it had brought them to tears.

"When isn't a day with Miss Rose an adventure?" Allison said smiling fondly in Rose's direction.

"I cannot believe you all kept this from me. You know I wouldn't have turned you and your buddies away." Kat chided her brother. She was deliberately ignoring the question Derek had asked her about Josh calling her.

"What fun would that have been? Of course, I didn't know that you were going to attack me with a bat," Blake said. He still had a red spot on his face where the bat had struck him.

Kat started yawning, "Well as much as I would love to stay in here with everyone, I am going to go to bed. I have to get up early in the morning; got a lot to do. Nice to meet you Shawn; Travis and Reggie nice to see you again. I take it that everyone knows where they are sleeping and where the bathrooms are so I am assuming you don't need me for anything."

"You're going to bed already? You could stay up a little longer and visit," Blake said.

"Well, if I heard you right, I'm gonna have to put up with you for a while so I am sure we will have plenty of time to talk," Kat said as she headed to her room.

CHAPTER TWENTY-FOUR

Kat rubbed her eyes trying to wipe the sleep from them. When her alarm had went off, she had been tempted to shut it off and then go back to sleep. She needed a good strong cup of coffee and then she would head for the shower. The long day from the day before was taking its toll on her.

She made her way down the stairs and toward her kitchen. The closer she got to the kitchen the more she thought she must still be dreaming; the wonderful smell of coffee was getting stronger and was assaulting her senses.

"What are you guys doing up?" Kat asked.

Upon walking into her kitchen, she found Blake, Shawn and her grandma all sitting at her kitchen table; all of them with a cup of coffee in front of them. Her grandma also had a cup of orange juice in front of her.

"Catching up, sleepyhead," Blake said grinning at her.

"Drinking my breakfast," her grandma said.

"You drinking your orange juice and vodka already grandma?" Kat said shaking her head.

"What do you mean already? She hasn't stopped drinking her vodka since she started in on it last night." Blake informed her, "I talked her into a cup of coffee but I don't think she has even had one drink of it yet."

"Wait a minute, are you telling me that none of you have been to bed yet?" Kat asked her eyes going wide.

"Nope, I stayed up talking to granny here and time just slipped away." Blake said taking another drink of his coffee.

"I needed to get my nutrients," her grandma said gesturing toward her drink. "I think I lost a bunch yesterday with all the excitement."

"I'm gonna go get a shower, it's too early in the morning for this. Save me some coffee please." Kat said over her shoulder as she headed back upstairs.

CHAPTER TWENTY-FIVE

Kat got out of the shower, dried herself off vigorously and started combing out her long hair. Her thoughts drifted to the three people downstairs in her kitchen. It was really good to see Blake again, but with him and his buddies staying at her house she didn't think her parent's Anniversary Party would get here quick enough.

She thought about her grandma and the more she thought about the last couple of days, the more she should have known something was up. Her grandma was something else but even for her the last couple of days had been crazy. Rose was known to lolly-gag around talking to people and could get side-tracked easily. In fact, the only time here lately that she had got in a hurry was when they were at the diner and she thought Charlie was going to come and talk to them after he had bought their dinner. The thought of the look that had been on her grandma's face caused a big grin to come over Kat's face.

She finished her hair, got a pair of jeans on and grabbed a t-shirt. Her thoughts strayed toward the third person that was in her kitchen. Shawn had been quiet, not that the others had given him much of a chance to speak. He had gorgeous blue eyes and an easy smile that Kat had noticed last night even with everything that had been going on.

She stopped and looked at herself in the mirror. It had been a long time since she had been in a relationship. She pushed the hair out of her eyes and scrunched her nose up. She very seldom wore make-up; she just didn't like to mess with it. She had been told that she had natural beauty and that she didn't need it. Of course, the people that had told her that were either her family or guys that had been trying to get in her pants. She shrugged her shoulders and sighed. It didn't really matter what she looked like; she was too busy to be in a relationship.

She went down the stairs and smelled something wonderful. She walked into her kitchen and was amazed to see Shawn standing at her stove cooking an omelet. Blake and Rose still sat at the table.

"Blake please tell me that you don't have him cooking you breakfast. You are a big boy and perfectly capable of cooking your own food," Kat scolded him.

"Well, I could tell you the same thing," Blake smirked. "He is not cooking for me or Granny. He has been slaving over that hot stove for you."

Blake started laughing at the look on his sister's face.

"I just thought that since the rest of us are not going to be working and are staying at your house being bums, that I could help out by cooking for you on occasion. I thought maybe breakfast would be a good way to start your day after the day you had yesterday." Shawn said smiling at her.

Kat just stared dumbly at him, although she couldn't help but notice how straight and white his teeth were.

"I told you Kathryn that you should have straightened your cabinets. Now you have a good-looking man fixing you breakfast. He's going to think you are a slob." Rose slurred.

Kat ignored her grandma's comment and returned Shawn's smile.

"Thank you for fixing me breakfast. It smells delicious. You didn't have to go to all this trouble though," her cheeks turned a little pink as she looked at him.

"No trouble at all. I enjoy cooking. It's the least I could do with you letting us stay here," he said as he put the omelet on a plate.

"She didn't have much of a choice," Rose said. "I would have been ecstatic to come home to see a bunch of good-looking guys in my house. Not to mention waking up to have this gorgeous man in my kitchen cooking for me. I would have had to find out if I had paid for some male companionship after I had drunk too much the night before. The only thing that would have made it better is if he was standing in front of my stove with nothing on but an apron," Rose said winking at Shawn.

"Actually, Grandma, you wouldn't have had to pay for some male companionship; you could have just called Charlie," Kat said as a big grin came across her face.

"Oh hell!" her grandma exclaimed. "I do not want to talk about that old pervert."

Kat started laughing as she sat down at the table and Shawn put the omelet in front of her.

"Ole Charlie still hot to trot for you? Why don't you just go out with the poor guy?" Blake asked looking at Rose with a big grin on his face.

"Because he just wants to get me drunk and take advantage of me!" Rose exclaimed.

"What's wrong with that? Maybe if you got a man and got laid you wouldn't be drinking so much vodka," he teased.

"If I got me a man, I would probably be drinking more vodka!" Rose grumbled.

Kat shook her head and looked at Shawn. "Please excuse my family, they do not have any manners. This is very good by the way," she said as she took another bite.

"How soon are you leaving for Grumpy's Palace?" Blake asked her. "I thought maybe I could come to work with you."

"You haven't got any sleep yet. Besides you can't be seen there since Mom and Dad do not know you are home. You stay here with Grandma and your buddies and take it easy. Go fishing or something. Don't let Grandma get in the hot tub naked though," Kat said standing up taking her empty plate to the sink.

"She is such an old stick in the mud." Rose said looking at Shawn. Her remark brought another smile to Shawn's face.

"Make yourselves at home. Go fishing, get the boat out, the Razor may need gas but you all can get it out. Don't let Grandma drive the Razor. The last one I had she ran off of my dock and into the pond. I will see you all later; get some sleep. I do not know what time I will be back home. If you need anything get a hold of Derek. Remember Blake, you cannot be seen here," Kat said grabbing her purse and keys off of the counter as she headed out the door.

"Don't worry Katherine, I will take care of the men folk for you!" Rose hollered at Kat's retreating back.

CHAPTER TWENTY-SIX

Kat put her head in her hands and sighed. She had planned on getting done early so she could be home early for a change. Since Blake had been at her house, she had been unable to be home before 8-9 pm. She had to go to the caterers to go over the menu again; for some reason her order had gotten mixed up.

She had went to the florist to order flowers after having talked to them the week before, only to find out that due to a system issue the coolers that had housed the flowers had went down over the weekend. Normally this would have been noticed and fixed before the flowers had been affected but the owner had a wedding over the weekend and had closed the shop up early on Friday and had not been back until Monday morning. This had resulted in Kat having to call around to other florists to get the flower arrangements she wanted.

On top of all the mishaps regarding the party, she had fallen behind on her own work. They had been short staffed a couple of nights in a row and she had to fill in behind the bar. She could have called Derek or Megan to come fill in but she knew that they needed to have time to themselves.

She had also been checking into getting a grill set up. Grumpy's Palace was a pretty good-sized establishment. It had several offices, not that any of them ever got used besides hers. There was an employee lounge set up, a room that was closed off for conferences and of course the bar itself. The bar took up quite a bit of space but there would still be plenty of room to put a grill on the opposite wall. Of course, today had been the day that the contractors had contacted her and had wanted to come into the club to look things over. Before she did any construction work she had to finish waiting on a few more permits to get approved.

In between getting all her running done and trying to get caught up on her work, the last couple of days had numerous phone calls from Blake, Derek and Grandma. Apparently, her Grandma had not been on her best behavior. She felt like she was the adult that everyone came too to tattle on everyone else.

"How in the hell do you deal with her?" was the first words out of Blake's mouth on the last phone call. She had to smile at the thought of her Grandma and Blake together again and she was glad that she had been at work while all of this was going on. At least her Grandma had finally laid down and took a nap.

The phone rang again and Kat let out a loud sigh, no wonder she wasn't getting any work done. Her Grandma's voice answered Kat when she answered the phone.

"Kathryn, I got an important question for you."

"I am sure that it can probably wait until I get home," Kat said.

"Nope, it can't wait. We are all sitting at the kitchen table having a conversation and we all decided that we need your opinion."

"Fine, what is so important that you all have to call me at work and cannot wait until I get home?" Kat said dreading to hear what the "important conversation" was about.

"Well, your brother Blake believes that fake boobs are better than real ones because they stay where they are supposed to and don't sag."

"Actually sis," Blake's voice broke in, "I said that if I am laying on the bed naked with a girl, I don't want to worry about laying on one of her "girls" like Granny likes to call them. Not to mention that when I'm looking at her, I want her "girls" to be on her chest where they are supposed to be and not in each armpit."

"Wait a minute, are you all calling me to ask my opinion on fake and real boobs? Seriously!" Kat felt her temper rising. "This is the "important conversation" that couldn't wait until I got home?"

"Now Kathryn, you need to hear my side of this disagreement," Rose said.

"I imagine that you will not leave me alone until I listen to you. I'm not going to get any more work done tonight, am I," Kat said sighing in frustration.

"Nope. You need to get your butt home. Whatever you got to do can wait till tomorrow," Blake said.

"Wait Kat, before you hang up you need to hear the rest of this," Rose insisted.

"Sure, go ahead; not that I have much choice," Kat muttered.

"Ok, I told Blake that fake boobs are too hard and that real ones are better. If a guy wants to lay his head on a woman's chest, he doesn't want to lay it on a hard surface, but on a softer surface."

"She did offer to show us her boobs as a visual aid," Derek's voice cut in, "I told her that no one here wanted that type of visual aid and if she did that, we would all be scarred for life!"

"And I told her that if she did show off her "girls" that

everyone that thought real boobs were better than fake ones would change their minds real quick like," Blake said laughing.

"I just thought a visual aid would have helped. I told them they could find an old lady with fake boobs to compare them with mine. I guarantee that mine would look better. I even offered to let Shawn lay his head on my girls to feel how soft they were."

"Grandma!" Kat gasped.

"What? It's not like I could ask Derek or Blake to do it. That would have just been wrong," Rose said surprised by Kat's reaction.

"Asking anyone to put their head on your breast is wrong," Kat scolded her.

"She got mad at me when I told her that Charlie would probably do it," Blake said laughing.

"Alright, I'm gonna get off of here so I can get stuff put up and then head home. What's for supper? I'm starving," Kat said.

"I don't know. What are you fixing Shawn?" Blake hollered.

"Oh, come on, Shawn you don't have to do any cooking. I'll just grab a couple of pizzas," Kat said.

"I don't mind Kat. I like to cook," Shawn's voice came over the phone.

"Ok, after the breakfast you fixed the other morning and all the food you have saved for me the last couple of days, you are not going to hear any arguing from me," Kat said laughing.

Rose and Blake both started to say something at the same

time but Kat cut them off.

"I'm hanging up now," she said and then hung up the phone before anyone else could say another word.

CHAPTER TWENTY-SEVEN

"Oh, good grief! If I take you to work with me will you stop bugging me about it? I swear Blake, if someone sees you and Mom and Dad find out you're here and their Surprise Party gets ruined I will knock you out, throw your big ass in my boat and then throw your body overboard in the middle of my pond!" Kat said.

Blake looked behind him at his butt, "You seriously think I have a big butt?"

"I'm ranting and raving and all you get out of it is that I think your butt is big? You are an idiot."

Kat's ranting just got her another big smile from Blake.

"I will behave myself. I'm just tired of staying here. Everyone else can leave since they are not really known around here. Don't get me wrong sis, you have a beautiful place; I'm just needing a change of scenery."

Kat sighed, "I understand, I really do. I just don't want their party to get ruined. I've spent a lot of time trying to get this all done."

"Have you heard from Mom and Dad lately?" Blake asked.

"Been a couple of days. I'm just glad Grandma hasn't been around when they have called. They are supposed to be back from their vacation soon," Kat started getting all her stuff ready to go to work.

"If you're going with me you better get ready to go."

"All I gotta do is get my shoes on. I don't think I need anything else." Blake said.

Kat turned around to go back upstairs and almost ran right into Shawn. If he hadn't of put his hands up and grabbed her, she would have run right into him.

"You trying to run away from Blake?" Shawn asked grinning.

"Not this time. He is finally going to go to work with me. I doubt if it shuts him up and I will probably regret it but I'm tired of him asking," Kat said smiling.

"He finally wore you down, huh," Shawn said smiling. "I wondered who would give up first, him asking you or you telling him no."

"Well, this time I gave in first," Kat said grinning at Shawn as she moved by him to head upstairs.

When she came back downstairs, Blake and Shawn were both talking in the kitchen. The conversation abruptly ended as she walked in. Kat was too distracted with her thoughts to even notice that their conversation had stopped.

"Would you care if I tagged along?" Shawn asked. "I could try to help you keep an eye on Blake."

"Sure, that's fine. I really don't know what you two are going to do…. unless you both plan on getting hootched up. What about Reggie and Travis? I haven't seen them too much." Kat said as she sat down to get her own shoes on.

"If you wouldn't work so much, you might actually get to visit more," Blake said accusingly.

"It won't get done by itself," Kat reminded him.

"Reggie has been spending a lot of time with Allison. If Travis isn't visiting with Liz, Derek, Megan, or Grandma, he is usually fishing on your pond with Shawn."

"Are you two ready to go? Reggie is a nice guy. I'm glad Allison is spending time with him. Hopefully Travis is not being bored." Kat said grabbing her keys out of her purse.

"You going to let me drive your Mustang?" Blake asked.

"What kind of stupid question is that? I know how you drive and there is no way you are driving my car," Kat said shaking her head at him.

"You are a wise woman," Shawn said as he got in the backseat.

"I don't need any lip from you," Blake said as he crammed his long frame into Kat's car.

CHAPTER TWENTY-EIGHT

Several hours later Kat was trying to get more of her stuff organized. Blake had been asking her questions all morning. He had asked about the new computer program she had installed, the construction and permits for the grill, the party arrangements and anything else that popped into his head.

Shawn had asked a few questions regarding the grill and Kat had warmed up talking to the guys about her ideas. Shawn and Blake both had suggested a few ideas as well. If everything went well, it was going to be a pretty good addition.

Kat yawned as she stood up and stretched; another cup of coffee was needed. She looked out her window and noticed that a light rain was falling. She walked over to her window to see if the rain was coming in. She had opened the window earlier since there was a good breeze outside. At the moment the rain was not coming in so she wasn't going to shut it just yet.

They had been there longer than she had thought looking at her watch. Maybe she would get to see a rainbow she thought to herself and smiled.

She opened her office door and headed to the lounge. Blake and Shawn were sitting at one of the tables playing a game of cards. They both looked up as she walked in.

"Decide to come out of your hole?" Blake asked. "Must be coffee time again. Maybe you should sit down for a bit; you look exhausted." Concern for his sister was in his voice.

"I got too much to do Blake. I made a list of stuff I wanted to get done today and I haven't even made it half-way through. If you two are tired of being here, I can run you back to the house." Kat told them.

"I can take care of them sis," Derek said walking into the lounge followed by Megan and Rose.

"The party just got here," Blake said smiling. "It's not time to go home yet!"

"Well, you all don't get to carried away. I need to get back to work." Kat said filling her coffee cup.

"Kathryn, would you mind accompanying me to the little girl's room?" Rose asked her.

Kat looked at her grandma and raised her eyebrows, "Sure, I guess I can."

"Thank you dear. I appreciate it," her grandma said.

Kat followed her grandma into the restroom, "Ok, what's up?" she asked her as she turned to look at her.

"Honey, I know you have a lot to do, but you look like you are about to drop from pure exhaustion. You have dark circles under your eyes and you are starting to worry us," her grandma said as she walked up to Kat and gave her a hug.

"I am fine Grandma," Kat said returning her hug. "I will be better once everything goes back to normal."

"Well, there are a lot of people here who could help you. You should take advantage of it. Don't be stubborn and think you have to do it all yourself. We can go on back in with the others; I just wanted to talk to you about that in private. Unless of course you want to talk about that sexy stud who has been cooking for you," her grandma said with a sly smile.

"Nope, we can go back out there and talk to everyone else. Besides, I need to get back to work. Being the end of the week, the club's probably going to get a little crazy." Kat said as they exited the restroom.

As they walked back into the lounge, Kat noticed that Blake was no longer sitting at the table with Shawn.

"Where did Blake go? He sneak back into the bar again?" Kat asked.

"Not sure where he went. He just got up and said he had to go do something and walked out." Derek said not meeting his twin's eyes.

"Derek, you better tell me now where he went. I know you know more about where he went than what you are saying. You are never able to look me in the eye when you are hiding something or your feeling guilty about something." Kat said crossing her arms over her chest.

Derek's eyes looked up at her and then looked towards the lounge door.

"Never mind, I will find out what he's doing on my own," she said as she uncrossed her arms and strode out of the room.

Kat stuck her head in the bar but there was no sign of Blake. The bar was definitely starting to fill up but as tall as Blake was, she was pretty sure that she would have been able to spot him from a mile away. As she turned around and started toward the offices, she noticed her office door was shut.

"Oh no he didn't!" she said out loud as she turned the handle only to find that the door was locked. "Blake, open this door up this instance!" Kat growled at the closed door.

"Nope, not going to happen. I know how to do your work. I did it for several years before you started doing it. Thank you for showing me how to work the new program by the way. You need to either go home and take it easy or go visit for a while. You are working yourself too hard. It is my job as the eldest to look out after you. Now what kind of big brother would I be if I let you work yourself to death." Blake responded.

"Blake, you little whistle dick, open my damn door!" Kat said getting more frustrated by the minute.

"That's not a very nice thing to say Kathryn," Rose said from behind her.

"Nope it's not Granny. She's hurting my feelings. This morning she said I had a big butt and now she's saying I have a little penis!" Blake said.

"Kathryn, where are you going?" Rose asked as Kat kicked the door and then stomped off. "He's just trying to help you out."

Kat whirled around to face Rose. "Did you bring me into the bathroom to get me away from him so he could sneak into my office?"

Kat was so mad she could feel her face turning red. Rose just looked at Kat and did not respond, which was all the response she needed. Kat turned around and walked out the door.

Derek and Rose both went out after her. Kat had walked out of the building and had headed right for her office window. Before anyone could stop her, she was pushing the screen in. The window was just tall enough that Kat had a little trouble jumping up onto the window sill to try to haul herself through.

Derek was the first to walk around the building and couldn't help but laugh at the sight of Kat's head in the window and her rear end hanging out.

"Now this scene looks familiar. Grandma, how does it feel to see someone else hanging out a window for a change?"

"Screw you Derek!" Kat snapped.

Derek and Rose saw Blake walk up to his sister. It looked like he was trying to help her get in and talking to her all the while.

"Blake you need to get out of my way," Kat said as she finished crawling through the window.

Derek and Rose watched Kat's back half disappear through the window. Once she was inside, they both headed back in at a quick pace, not wanting to miss out on anything.

CHAPTER TWENTY-NINE

"What the hell is wrong with you, locking me out of my own office?" Kat spluttered as she picked herself up off the floor.

Now sis, don't get your panties in a bind. Sit down so we can talk." Blake said.

"What is there to talk about? You took it upon yourself to decide that I am too stressed to work and locked me out of my own office!" Kat stormed.

Blake looked down at his sister. Under normal circumstances or if her anger had been directed at someone else, he might have laughed. With him being the object of her anger, there was no way he was going to laugh out loud; there was no telling what she would do to him.

He could tell that he may have over-stepped his bounds this time. She stood there glaring at him with her hands on her hips, occasionally pointing her finger at him as she continued to tell him that she was a big girl and was capable of taking care of herself. Her face was still red and her eyes shone brightly with her anger.

"Your right, I shouldn't have locked you out of your office. Everyone is worried about you though sis and I only had your best interests at heart. You are working late doing all the office stuff on top of filling in when needed in the bar. You have the grill project your working on so you are dealing with permits and contractors. When granny's mind wonders, you're the one that everyone calls to come take care of her cause she doesn't listen to anyone else. You are also planning Mom and Dad's party on top of everything else. If you weren't such a control freak you would let the people that care about you help you out."

Kat stared at her brother in astonishment, her mind taking in all that he had said. She went and sank down in her chair putting her head back.

"I never thought of myself as a control freak but I guess you're right. I had to have you point out all the stuff that I am handling right now. I guess your right though, I don't like anyone else to do my work. It is just easier to do it myself that way if something goes wrong I only have myself to blame," she finally said.

"Granted, Derek messed up ordering stock last time you let him so I can't blame you for not letting him touch your paperwork but he is pretty handy at other things. You are surrounded by family and friends who can and will help you. I doubt there is one person who knows you that wouldn't drop what they are doing and come help you. Hell, even Mom and Dad would come in and help you when they are home." Blake said pausing a moment.

"How about I help you with the permits and the contractors? I'm done with the job we were working on. The next one coming up is not a very big job. I could hold off on it or even send some of my guys to do it; that's the benefit of being the Boss," he said smiling at her.

Kat looked at Blake and smiled, "It's good having you around. No one else would have went to the extreme of locking me out of my own office. You're such a goof ball most of the time that it is easy to forget that you actually have a working brain in there."

"I doubt if anyone else would have went to the extreme of pushing in their office window screen so that they could get back into their office they were locked out of," Blake said chuckling.

"I don't know about that. I bet Grandma would have," Kat said laughing with her brother.

"You are probably right," his smile slipped a bit "We good? You're not mad at me anymore?" he asked.

"No, I'm not mad at you anymore. If you ever do this to me again though, no matter how much I would like to be an aunt, you will not be the one to give me a niece or nephew. Understand?" Kat said smiling.

"Understood loud and clear!" Blake said giving her a mock salute.

CHAPTER THIRTY

Kat put her finger to her lips and crept toward her office door. She quietly unlocked her door and yanked it open. Derek and Rose stumbled and almost fell when it opened. Behind them Megan, Leon and Shawn all pretended to be working or just walking by when the door happened to open.

"I'm really surprised to see you two standing outside the door. If I didn't know any better, I would say you were eavesdropping on our conversation but I know that can't be right cause our family is not the least bit nosy," she said mockingly.

"It's not what you think. Grandma stumbled and almost fell. I was holding onto her helping her out." Derek insisted.

"That's lame even for you Derek," Blake chuckled.

"You should know better than try to lie to her about something so obvious. She's not an idiot boy," Rose said. "We were listening to your conversation just so we wouldn't have to ask you two what was said."

They all started laughing at Rose's statement.

"So, you are actually going to let some of us help you?" Derek asked. "I know, I know, I still am not allowed to do the paperwork. Leon and I are both able to be here for deliveries. I am sure Liz, Allison or Megan can help out with some of your stuff."

"I said I would accept help, but don't expect me to just give up everything," Kat said.

"We will take what we can get," Blake said giving Derek a warning look when he looked like he was going to argue with his twin.

"I'm sorry if I put extra stress on you Kathryn." Rose said. "Blake is right though; you are the only one that I will listen too. You just know how to handle me and the situations I put myself in."

Kat went and gave her grandmother a hug, "You know I wouldn't have you any other way."

"I meant to ask you sis, did you invite Grandma and Grandpa James?" Blake asked with an angelic look on his face.

"Please tell me you didn't invite that old snooty witch!" Rose said looking at Kat.

"Well Grandma, they are Mom's parents. It wouldn't be right to not invite them to their only daughter's Anniversary Party." Kat said shooting Blake an annoyed look.

Blake pretended not to notice the warning look in his sister's eyes. "Don't tell me you two still don't get along with each other," he said in mock horror.

"You know dog gone well that we don't get along. It is not likely to change anytime soon." Rose said.

Leon walked up to the group. "Megan is taking care of the bar right now. I think we are going to have a good-sized crowd tonight. I forgot about you and Fern having that little tiff going on," he said looking at Rose.

"Tiff? I guess that is one way to put it," Rose snorted.

"What started that anyway?" Derek asked.

"She said she knew more about cooking and having parties than I did. I told her that people would have more fun at my parties because I didn't act like I had a stick up my butt," Rose said. "She is nothing but an old stick in the mud who wouldn't know what fun was if it came up and slapped her on her uppity old ass!"

"Now Grandma, we all know that you two are total opposites but she is Mom's mom so they are coming and you will behave yourself. Besides she has loosened up some since the last time you two were around each other."

"Sorry kids, I know that they are your grandparents too. I just don't like to have someone act like they are better than me," Rose sulked.

"It is kind of hard to believe that her and Grandpa Harold are married. He's always been so down to earth and she has been well, not." Derek said.

"You know she probably wouldn't be so snotty to you if you wouldn't do stuff on purpose just to annoy her." Kat said.

"Yeah, like the time you went swimming and decided to "borrow" some of her clothes?" Blake snickered.

"Well, I was told that I couldn't go skinny dipping so I thought it would be ok to wear some of her clothes," Rose said.

"I think what really got her going is when Grandpa Harold told Grandma Rose that she could keep them since they looked better on her than Grandma Fern," Blake chuckled.

"I tried to give them back to her when she threw her fit but she told me to keep them," Rose said.

"That's because you started taking her clothes off in front of everyone!" Kat said laughing.

"I was only doing what she asked me to do," Rose said with a mischievous grin.

"Well, I am sure that is all it was then, you just being compliant," Blake said laughing.

"Well of course!" Rose said grinning back at her grandson.

"I don't think she will ever forgive you though for what you had me call her when I was little," Derek said grinning, "I thought she was going to stroke out when I went up to her and called her Grandma "Up the ass". I was trying to say Grandma "Uppity ass", which is what Grandma told me to call her."

"That was pretty priceless seeing her mouth drop open. She was so mad that her face was red. If I knew that would have shut her up like it did, I would have told you to call her that sooner." Rose said grinning.

"I was four!" Derek said.

"You know Kat, I've been thinking. I bet Mom and Dad wouldn't think anything of it if I told them we finished up early and decided to come for a visit."

Kat sighed, "I'm actually surprised you haven't said something like that sooner. I guess it will be alright."

Blake let out a shout of joy and picked his sister up spinning her around.

"Awesome! Since you have decided to let other people help you, that means that you can do some socializing." Blake said grinning at his sister.

"Fine," Kat said letting out a sigh, "Now put me down you big lug."

"Ok, kids, party time is here but you all are still getting up to go to church tomorrow morning," Rose said, "that includes all of your buddies Blake,"

"Of course, Granny!" Blake told her as he hugged her and headed out to the bar.

CHAPTER THIRTY-ONE

Kat wiped the tears from her eyes. She had been laughing so hard she had tears going down her face and her stomach hurt. She had forgot how much fun it was when they all got together.

Derek, Megan and Leon all took turns taking care of the customers. They had all ganged up on Kat when she had got up to help. Someone had called Allison and Liz and they both had showed up with Travis and Reggie. Once they had all arrived, they had also helped with the bar and with taking people home.

Kat had been uncomfortable just sitting there letting everyone else work but eventually she had relaxed. Shawn had sat by her, laughed with her and they had gotten to know each other better.

"I'm telling you I can hula hoop longer than you can!" Rose said.

That statement got Kat to laughing again. Rose and Blake had been arguing about who could hula hoop the longest. She could not remember how that conversation had started but for some reason neither one of them could let the subject drop.

"I'm telling you that I can do it longer than you because you would throw your hip out!" Blake said again for the hundredth time.

"Ok, that's enough. I'm tired of hearing about this." Leon's wife Cindy said. "I think we have a hula hoop in the SUV from Tracy's talent show that was like a month ago. I am going to go get it and you two are going to do this!".

"Now?" Blake asked.

"Yes now" she said as she got up from the table and walked to the door.

"What's the matter boy, you all talk and no show?" Rose taunted him.

"Bring it Granny!" Blake hollered.

Minutes later Cindy walked back in with a hula hoop that was covered in glitter.

"Oh, this is getting recorded and put on Facebook," Liz said getting her phone ready.

"I'll let you go first Granny, you know the whole ladies first or age before beauty thing," Blake said grabbing his beer and finishing it off.

"Better get you another beer boy; you are going to need all the help you can get." Rose said as she got out of her chair.

Kat leaned toward Shawn, "I think they have both had enough to drink to make this interesting. Grandma may just throw her hip out but I don't think she will feel it till tomorrow."

Shawn started laughing, "Blake is all arms and legs so it would be funny watching him without booze but adding booze to the mix, this should be quite the site. Liz was right; this needs to be recorded," he said taking his phone out of his back pocket.

"My battery is about dead. Would you mind sending the video to my phone?" Kat asked.

"I guess that is one way for me to get your phone number," Shawn teased.

Kat felt her cheeks grow warm, "All you had to do was ask me for it. I would gladly have given it to you," Kat's hand went to her mouth, "Oh my goodness! Did I just say that outloud?"

Shawn's grin got wider as he handed her his phone, "Would you give me the honor of putting your phone number in my phone?"

"Of course," Kat said smiling at him as she put her phone number in his phone.

"Miss Rose, why are you taking your shoes and socks off?" Megan asked.

Rose had leaned against the bar and was taking her shoes and socks off. Leon and Derek had moved some of the chairs out of the way so the two would have plenty of room. Derek had mentioned to Leon that it probably would help to move as much stuff out of the way as possible since the possibility of them both falling would be extremely high.

"So I can get a better stance for my hula hooping," Rose said putting her arms in the air and swinging her hips as if she was already hula hooping.

"Careful Granny, I don't want you to throw your hip out before we even get started," Blake said teasingly.

"Don't you worry about my hips, they will be just fine. You better figure out how you are going to explain to everyone how you got beat by your Granny hula hooping after Liz posts it on that there Bookface," Rose said grinning.

"Bookface? You mean Facebook?" Derek said laughing as he came walking up to the group.

"Whatever it's called, he better get to figuring out what

excuse he is going to use," Rose said grinning.

"Enough yacking, you two need to get this party started!" Derek said.

Rose smiled and grabbed the hula hoop. After several attempts and a few curse words she got her rhythm down.

"Look at her go!" Kat said.

Shawn let out a loud whistle and a few other people let out some cat calls as Rose continued to hula.

"The only reason why she is able to keep doing it is because she has her tongue sticking out. That is how she is maintaining her balance," Blake said. "That should be considered cheating. Get your tongue back in your mouth!" Blake shouted at Rose.

Rose looked at him, grinned and then stuck her tongue out. As soon as she stuck her tongue out, she lost her rhythm causing the hoop to drop.

"I call interference! Do over!" Rose shouted.

"Oh no, my turn now," Blake said.

He went and reached down for the hula hoop and lost his balance. If Derek hadn't been standing there he would have fell flat on his face.

"Your off to a great start boy!" Rose hooted.

"I didn't have my tongue sticking out so my balance was off," Blake insisted.

He stood up and attempted to get the hula hoop going around his hips to no avail.

"Oh my!" Kat said, "You look like a drunk caveman!"

"Try sticking your tongue out Blake." Shawn hollered.

"Well shit," Blake said as he failed yet again to get the hula hoop going. He then put the hula hoop on his arm and started swinging it while his tongue was sticking out.

"Whoohoo," he shouted, "take that Granny!"

"Are you a simpleton or what? That's not how you do it." Rose said.

"Grandma's the winner!" Kat chuckled "I knew she would win."

"Whatever, you think you are so smart. Why don't you try it Miss Smarty Pants?" Blake said scowling.

"You just didn't have your tongue in the right place my friend," Leon said smacking Blake on the back.

"Come on Kat, get out there and show them how it's done!" Liz cheered.

"Fine," Kat said as she got up away from the table. She took the hula hoop away from Blake and went to the clearing.

"Been awhile since I did this," Kat muttered. The first time she tried it she failed but the second time she got it going smoothly. "Take that Big Brother!" she said smiling.

"That's my girl!" Rose hollered.

Kat grinned at her grandmother while keeping her rhythm.

"Hey Shawn, you watching Kat? She can really move her hips can't she!" Rose hollered at him.

"Oh yeah, I'm watching her. She definitely knows how to move her hips." Shawn hollered back at Rose while keeping his eyes on Kat and grinning broadly.

Kat felt her cheeks flush and faltered in her rhythm.

"I think you got her flustered Shawn," Derek said laughing.

"Well, I know what to do next time you and I have a competition," Blake said grinning widely, "I'll just have Shawn stare at you. Maybe I can get him to make suggestive comments or give you suggestive looks."

"Suggestive looks? Can guys do that?" Megan said, "I know us women can."

"Of course, we can," Blake said, "Show her Derek. It would just be too weird for me to show her my suggestive look. Besides I don't want to steal her away from you little brother," Blake said putting his arm around Derek.

"Yeah Derek, show me what you got," Megan said teasingly.

"I can't just do that on someone's whim, I have to be in the mood," Derek protested, "Can you do it just like that?" he asked Megan.

"Of course, I can," she said smiling.

"Prove it,"

Megan walked up to Derek, her back was to everyone else. The look she gave Derek must have done the job because he picked her up and slung her over his shoulder. Megan let out a squeal.

"Ok, you all, my woman is giving me suggestive looks so we are getting out of here. See you all tomorrow," he called over his shoulder.

"Don't forget we got Church tomorrow," Rose hollered.

Leon looked at his wife, "Are you going to give me suggestive looks too?" he said grinning.

She smiled at her husband, "How about this suggestive look?" she said as she closed her eyes and pretended to snore.

Leon started laughing, "That is definitely a look that I understand. Sorry to be a party pooper everyone but there are not too many of us sober people left. We all need to head home. It is close to 2 A.M."

"You are right. We all need to get to bed, especially if grandma is going to get us up to go to church tomorrow," Kat said.

After some grumbling they all started picking the place up. It took another hour for everyone to stop goofing off, pick up everything, wipe the tables down and figure out who was riding with who.

Rose made it very clear that she was going to Kat's house to make sure all the drunks got up for Church the next day. Eventually everyone got home and the club got locked up tight.

CHAPTER THIRTY-TWO

"Kathryn, get your butt up. Time to get ready for church."

"What?" Kat mumbled lifting her head up as she barely opened her eyes. The movement of her head made a groan escape her lips.

"Come on, get up lush. Shawn is getting breakfast made and the coffee on. Were you too lazy to take your clothes off last night? I'm sure that stud Shawn would have helped you out of them," her grandma's voice pounded through her head.

"Quit shouting. I do not want anything to eat. Don't you think Jesus will forgive me if I don't get up and go this time?" Kat said putting the pillow over her head.

"Oh no! I got everyone else up and saved you for last so you could get more beauty sleep. I even got that drunkard brother of yours up. The punk had the nerve to throw his pillow at me. I've already called Derek and Liz. Derek got an attitude with me but I told him that he better be there or I was going to stand out in his yard and yodel. He didn't drink last night so I don't know what his deal is," she muttered.

"Fine, I'm getting up. You don't look bad at all. I don't understand how you can drink as much as you do and never look hung over," Kat said groaning as she sat up.

"Years of practice my dear. You light weights have a long way to catch up with me."

"I am going to take a shower and then I will be down. Tell Blake if he starts doing crap to me intentionally because I am hung over, I will beat him when my headache goes away. Now I remember why I don't drink much!"

Kat could hear her grandmother's laughter as she made her way to her bathroom to shower.

Forty-five minutes later Kat made her way downstairs. Although she felt better, the idea of anything other than coffee made her belly roll.

She smelled the coffee first but not too long afterwards the smell of bacon assaulted her senses. Her belly immediately started rolling more than it already was.

"Gee sis, you look a little green. Not feeling very well?" Blake teased her.

"Shut up Blake. At least I didn't throw a pillow at grandma," Kat muttered.

"Here Kat, take a couple of these and sip on this Gatorade. This should help you feel better. I'll get you some coffee too but the Gatorade will help put electrolytes in you and make you feel a lot better." Shawn said coming up to Kat.

"Aww isn't that sweet! How come I didn't get this VIP treatment? I'm the one who brought you here." Blake said trying to put a hurt look on his face but failing terribly when he broke out in a grin, "Of course I'm not gonna kiss you like she did."

Kat started choking on the drink she had just attempted to take, "Blake! What the hell!" she spluttered. She sneaked a look at Shawn, her face flaming but he just had one of his magnificent smiles on his face.

"Well, it's about time you two did something. Did anything

else happen?" Rose asked hopefully.

"Grandma! Not that it is any of your business but we just shared a nice good night kiss." Kat said acting as if that simple kiss was not the best kiss she had had in a very long time.

"Well, if that was just a nice good night kiss, I am looking forward to another one," Shawn said looking at Kat with heat in his eyes.

"You two keep looking at each other like that and I don't know about the rest of the people in here but the sexual tension in here is gonna cause me to have an orgasm!" Rose said.

"Well, that just killed the mood," Kat muttered.

"You are a perverted old lady, Granny," Blake said shaking his head, "I don't want to hear anything more about how perverted Charlie is!"

"I don't even want to know where this conversation is going," Kat said getting up, "Time to get going. Is Derek meeting us here or at Church?"

"Nope, he is meeting us here. He came by while you were in the shower and got your Mustang keys," Rose said.

"Yeah, I meant to ask you about that. Why does Derek get to drive your car and I don't?" Blake asked.

"Well mostly because I was in the shower when he came and got my keys," Kat said drily. "You know if you would start driving your truck here instead of taking planes you would have your own means of transportation and wouldn't have to have everyone else chauffer you around.

"Speaking of the devil," Rose said as Kat's Mustang came

up her drive.

"Ok, everyone ready to go? I'm gonna get my water bottle and I'll be all ready," Rose said.

Fifteen minutes later, Kat was parking her car next to Derek's jeep. Allison, Reggie and Liz were already their waiting on them.

They made small talk with everyone and introduced Shawn, Reggie and Travis. As everyone was taking their seat in the back row, Kat found herself in-between Rose and Shawn. Blake, Megan and Derek sat on the other side of Rose while everyone else piled in next to Shawn.

A few times Kat had to give warning glances at Blake and tell her Grandma to behave but besides that everything went without incident until after the sermon. The Preacher's sermon was a great one, talking about the trials and tribulations that Job had went through. It always fascinated Kat that someone could go through all that he had went through without losing his faith.

As they stood up to sing one of the closing hymns, Kat's throat was a little dry so she asked her Grandma if she could have a drink of her water. Her Grandma handed her the water bottle and Kat took a big drink without noticing Blake's big grin and sudden interest and started gasping. The water in her Grandma's water bottle was not water but instead it was vodka.

Kat started gasping for breath and Shawn was trying to figure out what was wrong with her. Blake had sat back down and was laughing hard while trying not to make much noise. Since everyone was singing around them just a few people in front of them noticed the disruption.

Kat assured Shawn that she was fine once she was able to talk and then looked accusingly at her Grandma.

"You put vodka in your water bottle. Why would you do that and bring it to Church!" Kat hissed at her.

"Well Kathryn, I never actually said I had water. I just said that I needed to get my water bottle. I thought they may frown on me bringing the actual vodka bottle. Well, that is everyone except for Brother William; he would just expect me to share. That is not happening. The cheap ass can bring in his own vodka water bottle." Rose said sternly.

"I can't believe you did that!" Kat said.

"Oh, for goodness sakes Kat. I think you need another drink. It didn't bother you last night getting all hootched up."

"I wasn't in Church!" Kat snapped.

A loud rumble coming from the left of Rose made both of them stop and stare. Blake's face had gone red and a couple of seconds later both women were gagging.

"Good grief Blake! Is that you that has that dead sewer rat smell leaking out of you?" Rose said, "Maybe you should excuse yourself and go wipe."

"I couldn't help it Granny; it just kind of slipped out," Blake said grinning, "Besides, you always say that there is more room out than there is in."

Kat shook her head, "Blake you know you could have got up and away from everyone before doing that," she said as she put her hand over her nose trying to keep the smell out.

"I was afraid to move; how was I supposed to know it was

going to be that bad." Blake said shrugging his shoulders.

"Maybe cause when you drink you always have bad gas," Derek said drily.

"I guess I could have got up and walked in front of you and Megan. Of course, if I was in front of you two when it slipped out, I would have got hollered at for having my rear end discharging in someone's face." Blake said shaking his head. He threw his hands up in the air, "I was screwed either way!"

"It's not just when he drinks," laughed Shawn. "Don't try to pull that "how was I supposed to know it would smell that bad" crap. You never have any gas that doesn't smell like something crawled up you and died."

Blake leaned forward to respond to Shawn's comment when another rumble came from under him.

Rose and Derek lost it. Blake's face turned red once again. Rose and Derek both pulled their shirts up over their noses. They were laughing and Shawn was trying not to laugh out loud.

"Do we need to start carrying gas masks around when you are home?" Kat whispered.

"Sorry," Blake muttered.

"I don't know which is worse, Blake making us all gag or Grandma. giving me a drink of her vodka." Kat said. "I don't know what I am going to do with either one of you."

"I think Granny has me beat on that one," Blake said grinning, "What I did was not intentional. She intentionally brought her booze into Church."

"What difference does it make if I drink vodka in Church or not? I'm here aren't I? I'm not hiding anything. The Good Lord knows I like my vodka." Rose said. She did not seem to know what the big deal was.

The hymn ended just in time for everyone to hear Rose's words. Almost all of the people were now looking toward the back of the Church where they all sat.

"What is everyone looking at? I'm not sharing my vodka so everyone needs to get their own. This stuff is getting too expensive as it is and I am not sharing."

"Grandma, let's talk about this later. Church is almost over," Kat pleaded, feeling very uncomfortable with everyone looking at them.

"Now Kathryn, this is probably the most exciting thing that has happened for some of these people in here in a long time. Not everyone gets to hula hoop in a bar the night before and then drink vodka the next day in Church."

"Miss Rose, you need to sit down. You are embarrassing yourself and your family." Hope, Brother William's wife said in a very disapproving tone.

"Embarrassing myself and my family? If you think this is bad, you should have seen your husband last night. He was so drunk he was drooling and spilling his drink on everyone. I wouldn't be surprised if he peed on himself again. What about the time you celebrated your birthday at Grumpy's Palace? You got drunk, got on the table and danced and kept pinching my grandson's hind quarters!"

"You need to leave or sit down and shut up," Carol said. Kat sighed; no way was this going to end soon.

"Hello Whore of Babylon. Who asked you for your input?" Rose said.

"You're one to be calling someone a whore Rosy Green!" Carol snapped, "You are a whore and a drunk."

"Wait a minute, you can't call my Granny a whore. I can't argue with you about the drunk part but she is not a whore," Blake said standing up.

Everyone started talking at once.

A loud whistle from the front of the Church made everyone stop what they were doing. The preacher stood at the front of the Church and waited for everyone to quiet down.

"Thank you. I will not stand for anyone judging someone while they are in this House of Worship. That job does not belong to us. While I am glad to see you here Miss Rose, I am not very happy that you brought vodka in here. If the only way I can get you to come in here is for you to continue bringing vodka, then so be it; I am not going to stop you. I just ask that you keep your thoughts to yourself that are not appropriate; and that goes to everyone. If people have problems between one another and I can help, then please feel free to contact me after the services and I will gladly meet with you to offer my guidance. Now, everyone bow your heads so we can pray and ask for forgiveness of our sins and give the Almighty God our thanks for the blessings he has bestowed on us," the Preacher said as he bowed his head and started to pray.

After the prayer ended, the Preacher thanked everyone for coming. Kat and the rest of her family and friends could not get out of there fast enough. Everyone was quiet as they made there way to their vehicles and headed home.

CHAPTER THIRTY-THREE

Kat tossed her purse on the counter and put her keys on the shelf.

"Something smells good," Rose said coming into the kitchen. "Of course, a lot of stuff smells good after what we had to smell in Church."

"How many times do I have to apologize? I didn't have much choice," Blake protested.

"I put a roast on early this morning. I need to check it along with the potatoes and carrots to see if it is all done," Shawn said heading toward the crockpot.

"Sounds wonderful. I'm going to go into the other room and rest. Let me know when it's all done," Rose said heading toward the living room.

"Do you need any help?" Kat asked.

"It is pretty well done. I'm going to get some crescent rolls out and put them in the oven. As soon as they are done, we can eat." Shawn stopped talking and looked at Kat, "You don't mind me taking over your kitchen, do you? I've just been doing whatever I want without talking to you first. That has been kind of rude of me."

"Oh no! You have my permission to do whatever you want in here. I'm glad your making yourself at home; it's nice having these home cooked meals. Everyone would have starved or lived off of take-out if you hadn't stepped up," Kat said quickly.

"Besides, all you would have had to do is give her another kiss or turn your blue eyes her way and she would have let you do whatever you wanted," Blake said grinning and then proceeded to make kissing sounds.

"Shut up Blake," Kat muttered feeling her cheeks get hot, "I'm going upstairs to put some comfy clothes on. I'll be back down to help you when I am done." She said over her shoulder as she headed towards the stairs.

Moments later, Kat came back into the kitchen to find Shawn and Blake had already changed out of their church clothes.

"Wow, you both beat me!" Kat exclaimed. She had changed out of her black slacks and red dress shirt and had put on a pair of sweat pants and a t-shirt.

Blake and Shawn had both wore nice jeans with a dress shirt and now were in older jeans and t-shirts.

"Your just in time to help with the crescent rolls," Shawn said smiling at her.

"I can help too," Blake said making his way over to the counter where the other two were.

"Only if you promise to go into the other room if you even feel the slightest hint of gas passage coming," Shawn warned his friend, giving him a stern look.

"Fine!" Blake said.

They all three worked side by side as they put 4 containers of crescent rolls on two baking sheets. Occasionally, they would tease each other about the shape of a crescent roll. They talked about the club and the upcoming Anniversary Party.

"Derek and Megan are here," Rose shouted.

"Leave it to Derek to show up when everything is about done," Blake said shaking his head.

"Something smells good. Smells like we are just in time for lunch," Derek said coming through the garage door.

"It does smell good," Megan said. "But if you don't have enough, we can get something later. I hate just inviting ourselves."

"Nonsense, you are always welcome to whatever I have Megan. Derek knows this," Kat said giving the other woman a hug.

"I made sure to fix a lot of food," Shawn said reassuringly.

Within minutes everyone was seated around the table. Allison, Liz, Reggie and Travis had all made plans to eat in town which left Kat, Shawn, Rose, Blake, Derek and Megan.

"Kat, I meant to ask you if you had any plans this Wednesday. I need to go to the doctor for my check-up. Liz has a meeting around the same time as my appointment. I'm not about to ask Allison; Reggie has been following her around like a love-sick puppy. I don't really want him to come to my appointment." Rose said.

"Sure, Grandma. Just a regular check-up? Nothing serious I hope," Kat said.

"Nope, gotta get my legs spread and my boobs smashed. Just a regular old check-up." Rose said taking another bite of her roast.

Blake and Derek both groaned as other people at the table

chuckled.

"Grandma, I really don't want the image of you laying down spreading your legs or getting your boobs smashed," Derek said. "Aren't you too old for that kind of check-up?"

"Now Derek, that is probably the only time that she gets to spread her legs and have a man between them to get rid of all the cob webs," Blake said.

"Your smart alecks! I may be old but I still have to have my lady parts checked every now and then. I will tell you right now Blake, I don't have any cob webs in there," Rose snapped. "I may be older than you but I'm not dead."

"So, you are sexually active then?" Blake teased her.

"That's none of your business!"

"Sure, I can take you Grandma. Next weekend is Mom and Dad's party so I will be a nervous wreck until then. I will be glad to get this over with," Kat sighed slumping down in her seat.

"Good thing I locked you out of your office and had you see the error of your ways. You would really be a mess if it wasn't for me," Blake said, proud as a peacock.

"Yes, old wise one; without you I would be lost," Kat smarted off.

Rose chuckled, "It's nice having you home Blake. Kat and you have always bumped heads but she does listen to you. By the way Kat, my appointment is Wednesday at 10:30. Does that time work for you?"

"That time will be just fine. You might want to call me around

9-9:30 just to remind me," Kat said.

"I'll remind you as well," Blake said sighing, "I don't know how you all ever make it with me being gone so much."

His remark sparked several groans and chuckles from the other people around the table.

CHAPTER THIRTY-FIVE

The middle of the week came quickly for Kat. Rose called her at 9:15 to remind her to pick her up. Rose had gone back home to her and Liz's house on Sunday evening. Derek and Megan had brought her home when they left. They had all told her that she didn't need to leave but she had insisted. She had stated that since she had been eating Shawn's cooking, her clothes were getting too tight. She figured if she went back home and had to fend for herself or had to eat Liz's cooking, she would lose a pound or two before Wednesday.

Kat gathered her purse and keys then left her office, closing the door behind her.

"Leon, I'm going to head out now to take Grandma to her appointment. Blake will be here hopefully by 11. He has been using my truck to get around, so far, he hasn't torn it up. I appreciate you coming in early like this. I'm sorry the contractor didn't give me a specific time. He just said anywhere from 8 A.M to noon.

"No problem, Kat. Tell Miss Rose I said "hello". I hope she behaves herself," he said smiling.

"You and me both," Kat said returning his smile.

Kat walked out the door to her Mustang to find that it was misting out. She sighed as she got in her car. Hopefully, today would be simple; go to her appointment and then run to Wal-Mart to get a few last things. Liz, Megan and Allison were all going to help her. She figured Grandma would help her by drinking and supervising. Friday they were all going to get some stuff ready but Shawn and Blake were going to be handling additional grill and contracting business for most of the day. Saturday, the day of the party, Blake, Derek and Shawn were all going to be there to help hang decoration. Travis and Reggie were going to stick around as well in case anything came up that they needed help with.

She felt a grin spread across her face as she pulled into her Grandma's drive. Her Grandma was already standing on the porch waiting on her. Rose seen her pull in and came down the porch to get in the car.

"Hi hon. Thanks again for taking me," Rose said sliding into the front seat.

"No problem Grandma. You know I would do about anything for you," Kat's voice trailed off when she got a good look at her Grandma.

"Grandma, what in the world do you have all over you?" Kat pulled out onto the road and headed toward Rose's doctor.

Rose looked over at Kat and scowled. "I used Liz's bodywash. Apparently, body wash now-a-days comes with glitter in it but they fool you by saying it makes your body "glimmer and glow"."

"I have never seen that much glitter on a person who used body wash before," Kat said openly staring.

"Actually, she had body lotion that was the same as the bodywash. I thought you were supposed to use them both together. Liz keeps telling me we need to get some of those LED lights to brighten the bathroom up. Guess I should have listened to her."

"Why didn't you take another shower?" Kat said

dumbfounded.

"Because I just got out of the shower 15 minutes ago. I was waiting until the last possible minute to take a shower so my never regions will be nice and clean. I didn't have time to take another shower." Rose grumbled.

"I am sure the doctor wouldn't have minded if you were a little late. Now he will probably ask you if you got a part-time job as a go-go dancer," Kat said laughing.

"Really? You think he would give me a discount if I offered to give him a personal dance?" Rose said.

"Well, I guess you could always ask him, but since this is a routine visit, you shouldn't owe him anything."

"I could build up credit for future appointments," Rose insisted.

"Well, we are here so let me know how that goes for you," Kat said pulling into the parking lot at the doctor's office.

"Sure thing, honey," Rose said getting out of the car.

Kat shook her head as the two women walked to the door.

Rose stopped at the desk to check-in while Kat took a seat in the waiting room. She heard Rose say something and the receptionist laugh. Rose finished checking in and sat down by Kat.

"I guess the glitter is pretty noticeable. Jennifer, behind the desk, took one look at me and got a funny look on her face. I told her that I had a late night at my new job as a go-go dancer and hadn't had time to get all the sparkle and bling-bling off. I told her that I was pretty sure I still had my boob tassels on."

Kat snickered and looked at her Grandma, as she put the magazine she had been looking at down. "You know with you around I don't need any of these magazines to keep me entertained."

The two women didn't sit there very long before the nursed called Rose to the back.

Kat waited patiently in the waiting room occasionally checking her phone to see if Leon or Blake had sent her any messages. She checked her list of stuff to do for the party and what she needed to grab from the store after her Grandma's appointment.

Loud laughter caused her to turn her head toward the receptionist's desk. Dr. Johnson, Rose's doctor, was standing up at the receptionist's desk laughing so hard he was wiping tears from his eyes. He noticed Kat looking at them and motioned her up to the desk. Believing she already knew what he was laughing about, Kat got up and walked over there.

"Before I start telling you what I'm laughing at, I want to reassure you that Miss Rose gave me permission to tell what happened. I believe her exact words were "I don't give a rat's ass what you tell 'em. Whatever floats your boat son!"

Kat shook her head and smiled, "Sounds like something she would say. I know you and your staff would never breach the confidentiality agreement with anyone. What did she do this time?"

"Why don't you come on back here so I can tell you. I know there are no patients in the waiting room but I think I would feel better telling you in my office." Dr. Johnson said opening the door to let her in the back and then leading her back to his office. His nurse, Sheila was with them.

"Sorry honey, I just got to listen to this story again and see your face when you hear it."

"That good, huh," Kat said taking a seat.

"I am sure you know about Miss Rose's ummm glitter problem?" Dr. Johnson asked.

"First thing I noticed this morning when she got in my car," Kat agreed.

"Well, Jennifer told me about Miss Rose's new job as a go-go dancer and that she wasn't sure if she removed her ummm tassels or not. Since I have known Miss Rose for years, I knew I could give her a hard time about it. Anyway, I came in and started laughing. The girls warned me but I was taken back by the amount of glitter on her. I had to ask her about the tassels."

Sheila smiled, "We did warn him. Of course, as long as she has been coming in here, we should know to expect the unexpected."

"She was sitting on the exam bed when I walked in and the first thing she said was "Hello doc. Let's get this over with. According to Blake you are in charge of getting all the cob webs swept out of there. I want a written statement from you saying there were no cob webs present. Smart aleck thinks he is funny." She got all comfortable and I proceeded to start the exam. Let me tell you, if you think she had a lot of glitter on her face, that was nothing compared to what she had down there."

Dr Johnson stopped talking and started laughing, "She told me that the sparkle down there was because she was part fairy and when she had gas or got excited, she would "poof some glitter out"!"

They all started laughing.

"That's all I wanted to tell you Kat. I have to get back to work now. Miss Rose was going to get mammogram done and you should be ready to go soon. Amber will take good care of her."

"Amber?" Kat asked puzzled, "What happened to Carrie?"

"She's on maternity leave. Hasn't Amber ever had to deal with Miss Rose?" Dr. Johnson asked.

"I am not sure," Kat admitted.

As soon as those words left Kat's mouth, they heard a commotion outside the door. Kat recognized Rose's voice but did not recognize the other woman's voice.

"You better get away from me you mean ole heifer!" Rose's voice rang out.

"Miss Davis, please get back in the room so we can finish your mammogram," the other woman's voice called out.

"Your crazier than bat shit if you think you are going to rough handle my girls again!"

Dr. Johnson opened the door to find Rose standing there with an angry look on her face. Another woman who made at least two of Rose stood by her with her hand on her hips.

"Dr. Johnson, this woman is being very difficult. All I'm trying to do is get her mammogram done and she is fighting me at every step," the woman said.

"Being difficult," Rose stormed, "My girls need to be handled gently. You might like rough foreplay but I do not!"

"I also asked her to go wipe some of the glitter off of her chest. She told me that I need to try some on my face and body to hide the "rode hard and put away wet" look. She then said that if I did that, I might get me a man or a woman to bed me which would get the old sour puss look off my face.""

"I was just trying to give her some friendly advice," Rose insisted.

"Ok, Sheila, would you go with Miss Rose and help her get her mammogram done? Amber, why don't you go take a break?" Dr. Johnson said.

"That's what you need, go have a HO-HO or a snack cake," Rose smarted off.

"Grandma, behave yourself. She was just trying to do her job." Kathryn scolded Rose.

"Well, I think she got confused and went to a S & M college or something. I believe she has a whole trunk full of whips and chains and is just dying to use them!" Rose fumed.

Sheila hurried up and guided Rose back down the hall.

Amber went toward the opposite side of the building from the direction that Sheila took Rose.

Once they had both left, Dr. Johnson turned toward Kat. "Never a dull moment when Miss Rose is around," he smiled at her, "I guess I will see you this weekend at the party," he said.

"I am so sorry Dr. Johnson. She can be difficult at times. I look forward to seeing you this weekend," Kat said as she headed back toward the door that led into the waiting room.

Once Rose was done, the ladies headed out to grab some

lunch. Thankfully they got out of the doctor's office with no more incidents.

The two ladies stopped at a fast food restaurant and enjoyed a quick bite to eat. Several people came up to talk to the two women; a lot of them stopped to let Kat know that they would be there for her parent's party.

"I bet you are looking forward to this party Kat. You've put a lot of your time into planning this."

"I am looking forward to it, mostly to just get it over with. I know that's a terrible thing to say. I just hope everything goes well. Mom and Dad have called me several times since they got back. I keep making up excuses to not stay on the phone long or I get them to talking about their trip. Once they start talking about their trip, I don't have to worry about talking myself," Kat said laughing.

Rose looked at her granddaughter, "You do not seem to be as stressed as you were. I am sure that Blake making you share responsibility with others has helped," Rose got a sly look on her face, "or could it be that young man that you have been spending so much time with has helped you relieve some of that stress?"

Kat felt her face grow warm. "I do enjoy spending time with him but we haven't had sex if that is what you're asking."

"Well, what the heck are you waiting for?" Rose demanded. "You should be dragging him to your room or sneaking into his room in the middle of the night!"

"Grandma, I am not in any hurry to go that way with our relationship. Besides as soon as the party is over I am sure that Blake and his buddies will leave again," Kat said. "It will sure be different having the house all to myself again."

"I imagine it will," Rose nodded in agreement.

"Well, I am ready to go if you are," Kat said gathering up their trash. "Do you want to go to Wal-Mart with me?"

"I think I will just go home if you don't mind. I am ready to go home and take a shower to try and get some of this "glimmer" off of me. I might even take a nap after that," Rose said heading toward the door.

"I don't blame you. If that place didn't have everything, I need right there in one place, I would stay away from it. You sure you want to get the "glimmer" off of you? Won't you just have to put more on tonight before you go to your new job as a go-go dancer?" Kat teased her Grandma.

"You have a point Kathryn. Maybe I should just take my nap so I will be all refreshed for tonight." Rose said smiling.

They got in Kat's car so Rose could go home and Kat could get her shopping done.

CHAPTER THIRTY-SIX

The day before the Anniversary Party found Kat, Blake, Derek, Rose and Megan standing in the Conference Room trying to work together to get everything organized.

"I still think that you need to arrange the tables to where they are touching side by side in a line instead of scattered all over the place," Blake said yet again.

"I have heard you say that a hundred times today already and I still think you are wrong," Kat argued.

"Well, I am getting tired of you two arguing about it," Rose grumbled.

"I agree with Grandma. One of you need to back down so we can figure out where everything is going to go," Derek said crossly.

"I have a suggestion," Megan said shyly.

"You two need to shut your traps right now so we can hear what sweet little Megan has to say," Rose said raising her voice.

Kat and Blake stopped arguing and all eyes turned to look at Megan.

"I was thinking maybe we can incorporate both ideas. We could put the tables side by side on this wall and have your Mom and Dad in the center and maybe all you kids, Rose and your Mom's Mom and Dad sit at those tables. The rest of the tables we can put strategically around the room. Kat, you said you had poster board that you were going to put pictures of them on. We could put those by both of these walls," She said motioning to walls on the right and left from where the rows of tables would be.

"That sounds like a great idea," Derek said, "Now can we get busy? If we have to wait until you two decide which one is giving up first, the party will be going and you two will still be standing where you are at now."

"That does sound like a good idea," Kat said and Blake shook his head in agreement.

The two brothers started moving the tables into a line on the wall that Megan had indicated.

Not too much time had passed before Shawn stuck his head in the door. He had been in the bar area helping Leon. "I'm supposed to let you all know that your Mom and Dad just pulled into the parking lot. Leon said he will keep them busy for as long as he can."

"What the hell Blake! I thought you said they were going to Terra Haute to go shopping," Kat said with panic in her voice.

"That's what they told me," Blake said.

"Now you two don't be getting your panties in a bunch. That is if your wearing any. I personally don't have any on today. There is nothing in here that shows that it is going to be a party for them," Rose said.

"Sure, we got this; just as long as these two don't blow it," Blake said glancing over at Kat and Derek.

"Yeah, because we are the ones that talk all the time," Derek said drily.

"Cause we are the ones to worry about," Kat added shooting her brother an irritated glance.

Blake didn't get a chance to respond as Shawn stuck his head back in the room. "Hey, I'm supposed to let you know that your parents are here. They said that you three need to get your butts out there and stop avoiding them."

The three siblings looked at each other all of them thinking the same thing: did their parents know about their upcoming party?

The all walked into the main room. Edward Davis had his mother's eyes and temperament but had taken after his father in most everything else. Blake had received his height from his father. While Blake stood at 6'6, Edward stood right behind him at 6'5. Edward's hair was dark with just a touch of grey in it.

Cheyenne Davis was still a very beautiful woman. Her light brown hair had been cut shoulder length and her hazel eyes sparkled with pleasure at seeing her children walk toward them.

"Pretty bad that we've been gone two weeks and we have to come to a bar to see our kids!" She said grinning.

"We do feel neglected," Edward chimed in.

"I think you both are full of crap," Rose's voice came from behind them. "When was the last time you came and visited your mother Edward James?"

"Hello Mother; imagine finding you in a bar," Edward said leaning down to give his mother an affectionate kiss.

"Keep that sass up boy and see what happens," Rose said smiling at her son.

"So, what brings you two here?" Kat asked giving her mother a hug.

"Well it seems like everyone has been too busy to come and see us, so we figured we would hunt you all down and give you a guilt trip over it. Is it working?" Cheyenne asked with a twinkle in her eye.

"How you doing princess?" Edward said as he engulfed his daughter in a hug.

"Doing ok," Kat said returning his hug. "Sorry, I haven't meant to ignore you both. Things have been crazy around here. You can blame me for keeping Blake away from you two as well. He has been a big help handling the contractors for me. Shawn's been a big help as well with the grill." She said smiling at Shawn. He returned her smile with a big one of his own.

"What am I? Chopped liver?" Derek asked with a hurt look on his face.

"Of course not! You are always a big help to me. Mom, Dad, you can blame me for Derek not coming over too," Kat said defensively.

"She has been a slave driver!" Blake said, "She has been making me get up with the roosters, won't feed me and hasn't paid me one dime!" he said sighing loudly.

"You are so full of crap!" Kat said. "Unless roosters have started cock-a-doodling after 10 am. I'm not about to pay you any money, in fact, if I remember right, you still owe me $250.00."

"Well, you do have to admit that you haven't been feeding him since Shawn has been the one doing all the cooking." Derek said with a grin.

Cheyenne raised her eyebrows, "How many guys you got living with you dear?"

Kat's face turned red, "For the most part, just Blake, Shawn, and Travis. Reggie has been staying at Allison's I do believe."

"Don't worry, I was staying there for a while," Rose spoke up.

"That is reassuring," Cheyenne said drily.

Rose chose to ignore her comment, "They have been behaving for the most part. I only know of one time that her and Shawn were sucking each other's faces."

"Grandma!" Kat exclaimed with a shocked look on her face, "Seriously!"

Cheyenne and Edward both looked at Kat and Shawn.

"Really? Do I need to get my shotgun out boy?" Edward said looking at Shawn.

"Dad!" Kat exclaimed at the same time that Shawn responded "No sir".

Cheyenne looked at her husband, "Now dear, he seems like a good boy. Let's give him a chance. Besides I have been waiting on grandkids for too long. I always figured one of the boys would give them to us first. Besides, if he hurts Kat, then you get the shotgun out after I castrate him." She said sweetly.

Shawn's face paled as he looked at Kat's parents. "I have no plans on hurting her. I'm letting her choose what path our relationship takes. She deserves to be treated like a princess."

"Thatta boy," Edward said beaming at him, "I won't say too much with Blake staying there too. I know he wouldn't let you near her if he didn't trust you."

"You will have to excuse us dear. We have always been over-protective when it comes to Kathryn." Cheyenne said smiling at him.

"It was real fun in high school. The poor boys I dated about peed themselves every time they had to come to our house. Between Dad having his guns out, Mom sharpening knives, Blake being Blake and Derek instigating, it's a wonder that any boy wanted to date me!" Kat chuckled.

"I don't know what the big deal is. Kat's a grown woman. If she wants to do the wild thing with Shawn, that is her business. I myself don't see what is stopping her from banging him every chance she got, in every room of the house and every position possible. Back when your daddy was alive, we done it every chance we got!" Rose said looking over at Edward.

"Ok, time to change the subject. I don't want to hear about your sex stories Mom. I was scarred for life after walking in the house and finding you two going at it on the couch." Edward said shivering, "I never sat on that couch again!"

"Not my fault you came home early from your friend's house; you were usually late getting home and almost never showed up early. If you knew all the places we got our freak on, you wouldn't have left your room." Rose sniffed.

The group all groaned which made Rose's lips curl up in amusement.

"How about you showing us the plans you have for your palace princess? I'm interested in seeing what all you have planned for it." Kat's Dad asked.

"Sure! Like I said earlier, Blake and Shawn have been a lot

of help," Kat said leading her parents over to where the grill would be. Blake and Shawn came along as well and pretty soon all three were showing their enthusiasm with the ongoing projects.

"Kat, do you want me to stay and help with the decorations?" Cheyenne asked.

"I thought you two were going to Terra Haute?" Kat asked trying to keep the panic and desperation out of her voice.

"Don't you even try to get out of going. You drag me around all the time to go places with you. You are not about to get out of going to Sears with me," Edward scolded her.

Cheyenne sighed, "Well let's get going then. I know they have more than just tools there, but I can only stare at tools for so long. You can spend an hour in one aisle! We are going to our favorite steakhouse, right?"

When the group started laughing, Cheyenne looked at them all with a puzzled look on her face, "Am I missing something?"

"Well, let's just put it this way; you wouldn't be allowed in if Kat and Grandma was with you!" Derek said laughing.

Kat and Rose took turns telling the events of that night. When they got done both parents had tears streaming down their faces.

"Good thing I look more like Dad; after going through all of that I'm sure the manager would lock the door if she seen you two or anyone resembling you two in the parking lot," Edward said shaking his head.

"It's a good thing that boy didn't try anything else or it could have turned pretty ugly." Rose said.

"What in the world were you thinking saying that crap to that boy in the first place about our Kathryn?" Cheyenne said, "You should know better than that!"

Rose rolled her eyes at her daughter-in-law, "I know, I know. I apologized already. I thought I was helping her out. This was before her and Shawn you understand. She wasn't making any effort on her own to find herself a man; your not the only one wanting babies around here." Rose turned and looked over at Kat, "Did that good-looking man from the party store ever text you?"

Kat felt her cheeks grow warm, "Actually he did but I told him that I had started seeing someone."

Rose looked at her granddaughter and smiled. "I'm glad you told him that. I think Shawn is better looking. I think you should keep his number though just in case things don't work out between you two; no offense Shawn."

"None taken Miss Rose," Shawn said smiling at the older woman.

"Ok, enough stalling woman, let's go!"

Cheyenne sighed and looked at her husband, "Fine, let's go get this over with," she grumbled.

After Cheyenne and Edward left, Shawn looked over at Kat and raised his eyebrows, "So are we officially a thing now?" he said with a twinkle in his eye.

Kat smiled, "Well, that depends on what you are wanting from me. We can talk about this later if you want to," Kat looked over at her brothers, "Do you think they suspect anything?" She asked changing the subject.

Blake looked at Kat and then back at Shawn, "You two can discuss your relationship now if you want to. I can be the guy who listens to both sides and then gives my expert opinion at the end."

Derek shook his head at his brother, "I don't know what makes you an expert. When was the last time you were in a relationship? Wait, forget I asked. If I get you talking about your love life, Grandma will start asking questions and making comments that I really don't want to hear." Derek looked at his sister, "It is hard telling sis. Sometimes they are sharp as tacks and other times they are preoccupied with other things and oblivious to what is going on around them. Since they were on there way to town, I think they were too preoccupied."

"Well, come on you young'uns. I'm not getting any younger and we need to get some work done," Rose said heading back to the Conference Room.

The rest of the afternoon was spent setting up the tables and putting up some of the poster board that Kat and Megan had decorated with pictures of the couple. Kat draped some tablecloths over the poster boards so that no one could see the pictures. The guys had all pitched in to get the decorations hung from the ceiling.

"There," Kat said, "I believe we are done for today. Tomorrow we can get the food and finish some last-minute touches such as getting all of the candles lit and the flowers on the tables."

"Grant still in charge of getting them here?" Blake asked.

"Yep, as far as I know," Kat smiled at her friends and family, "Thank you for all of your help. Let's all go sit down and relax for a while."

"Wow, did you just say that we all can sit down and relax?" Blake teased, "Done cracking the whip for today?"

"For today," Kat said smiling at her brother.

Shawn and Leon had been taking care of the bar. The bar itself gleamed from the polish that had been put on it. Shawn was pushing a broom while Leon was making a list of the spirits that needed replenished.

"Get everything done?" Shawn asked smiling at them.

"Pretty well, we got more stuff to do tomorrow"

"Let me know if you need any help from me. I am at your beck and call," Shawn said bowing at her.

Later that evening Kat sat on her dock. She enjoyed sitting there listening to nature and watching the fish get the bugs that were on top of the water.

"Mind if I join you?" a voice said from behind her.

She turned her head and smiled at Shawn, "Of course."

The two sat there for several minutes without saying anything; the silence between them comfortable.

"Your place is beautiful, Kat," Shawn said breaking the silence, "It is so peaceful here, well, at least when Blake is not around," he said grinning.

"I do miss just being able to relax. It has been ages since I just sat here and even longer since I went fishing in my boat. I'm glad that you all have been able to enjoy it," she said sighing.

"I am sure you will be glad to get this party over with and get the construction done at your club," Shawn said taking her hand.

"For the most part," Kat said enjoying the feel of his hand holding hers. "Will you be leaving next week? Blake said he is going to stay and send some of you guys to the next job." Kat continued to look out at the pond, not wanting Shawn to see the look in her eyes.

"Why, are you ready to get rid of me?" Shawn said only half joking.

"Of course not. I don't expect you to put your life and job on hold for me. I'm not going to lie and tell you that I won't miss you though," Kat said glancing over at him.

"What is going on between us Kat? I have never felt like this with anyone. I am so comfortable with you but I don't want to rush you into something that you are not ready for. If you want me to leave so you can sort your feelings out for me, I will go. If you want me to stay and help you out at Grumpy's Palace, I will gladly do so. If you want my help, I do not have to continue staying here. I can get a hotel in town to stay at. If you just want to stay friends for now, I will not argue with you," Shawn said quietly.

Kat laid her head on Shawn's shoulder and he put his arm around her pulling her close.

"I really like you and I am comfortable with you too. You haven't been here real long but any more it just feels natural having you around. I don't want to prevent you from going back to work." Kat sighed, "Blake keeps telling me that I need to live my life and take chances. If you want to stay, I would love to have you continue staying here. If you want to go back to work or stay here and get a hotel room, I will not stop you. If you stay and help with the construction on Grumpy's Palace,

I will pay you for your time. I won't feel so bad keeping you from work if I do that."

If Kat was going to say anything else, her words were cut off by Shawn's mouth being on hers. Minutes later they reluctantly broke their kiss; both of them breathing fast.

"I will stay here till you chase me away. I do not want to stay at a hotel and there is no way that you are going to pay me anything. Believe me, I do not need you to pay me. I am quite financially comfortable," Shawn said smiling.

"We will see about me not paying you, mister, that conversation is not over. I do feel better now that everything else has been settled," Kat said snuggling up to Shawn.

CHAPTER THIRTY-SEVEN

The day of the party started with sunny skies. Kat stretched in her bed after her alarm clock went off listening to the birds chirping outside her window. She smiled as she thought about her talk with Shawn the night before. She had not realized that she had been dreading his leaving until he told her he was staying; she had felt like a weight had been lifted off of her shoulders. Now if she could just get through today without stroking out, it would be a miracle.

Kat hurried up and got dressed, anxious to get everything taken care of. She went down the stairs to the pleasant aroma of coffee and cinnamon rolls.

"Shawn you are amazing!" she said as she walked into her kitchen. Blake and Shawn were both sitting at her kitchen table.

Blake looked up at his sister, "How do you know that I am not the one who made the coffee and cinnamon rolls? I know how to fix coffee and bake cinnamon rolls!" he said.

"I never said you couldn't do either one of those things I just know how lazy you can be. If you have someone else to do stuff for you, I do not see you volunteering to do anything," Kat said as she poured herself a cup of coffee. "Did you make the coffee and cinnamon rolls?" she asked him grinning.

"That is not the point. The point is I could have done those things but you automatically assumed that your boyfriend did it. What you call lazy I call smart," he said taking a drink of his coffee.

Shawn had been watching the two siblings' banter back and

forth. He shook his head at them and smiled.

"You two crack me up. Sorry Kat, the rolls are not homemade but straight out of a can."

"Another reason why it is not Blake providing the rolls. His rolls would have been packaged and ready to eat," Kat said taking a bite of her roll.

"Your right, that would have been the smart way of doing things. Again, that is being smart not lazy," Blake said grinning.

"So, what's the plan for today?" Shawn asked.

"Well, we have to finish decorating, the cake has to be picked up, the food has to be picked up and I have to go to IGA to get the ice cream. Hopefully everyone shows up before Mom and Dad get here. Grant has volunteered to spend the day with them to make sure we know where they are at all times. I want to make sure they don't run into any of us while we are getting stuff for the party."

"So, who is doing what because I know your not crazy enough to think you are doing everything yourself," Blake said.

Kat frowned at her brother, "Well, originally that is what I was going to do. Now, I am going to pick up Grandma and we are going to meet Derek and Megan to do some decorating. You two are welcome to come with me to help."

"You think you all are going to get it all done?" Shawn asked.

"Well, I have no choice! I will go get the cake around noon-1 o'clock, pick the food up around 4 and then go get the ice cream at IGA. While I am doing that Grandma will be bossing everyone around to get everything in place. Megan is going to make sure Grandma doesn't go all crazy. I actually told her that she is kind of in charge but to let Grandma think she is making all the decisions. Megan can get Grandma to believe she came up with an idea to do something when in reality it was Megan's idea." Kat chuckled.

"I thought all you girls were going to get your hair done or something," Blake said.

"Oh, crap! That's right," Kat sighed, "Allison, Liz, Megan, Grandma and me are all supposed to meet up at Lisa's shop to get our hair done around 1:30-2:00. I lost the vote on that one; I didn't care if I got my hair done but apparently everyone else does."

"Don't worry sis; everything will be just fine. If you need us to get the food or cake, we can do that. If you need us to decorate while your gone, we can do that as well," Blake reassured her.

"I know I can count on you guys I've just spent so much time trying to get everything ready. I just want everything to be perfect," Kat said. "Ok, here is what we will do. Everyone can help decorate and get stuff set up. We still have to put the candles and table decorations on; at least the tablecloths are already on the tables. I need to figure out where the cake and food is going to go. I need to make sure one more time that we have enough chairs and tables; if not then I will need to go into the basement to get more. I almost forgot, the flowers have to be picked up and the arrangements need to be put on the tables," Kat said putting her head in her hands.

"Everything is going to be alright; quit trying to be Superwoman. Shawn and I can get the food and the flowers. You just worry about the decorations, the cake and ice cream and getting your hair done. We got this!" Blake said giving his sister a hug.

"I will get things cleaned up in here if you want to get things ready to go," Shawn said as he started to pick up the plates and coffee cups.

Twenty minutes later they had everything loaded into Kat's trunk and were on their way to Rose's house.

"It's about time you all got here. I was getting ready to start walking," Rose grumbled when they pulled into her drive.

"Hold on a minute Granny and I will get in back with Shawn," Blake said getting out of the car.

"Just stay where you're at. I don't mind getting into the back seat with this hunk!" Rose said grinning. "Kat you may not want to look in your rearview mirror. I may be taking advantage of your man."

"Just don't wear him out Grandma. I need him to keep his strength and energy up; I'm going to put him to work." Kat said as she started to back out of Rose's drive.

"Hey! Wait!" Kat stopped the car when she heard Allison's voice.

"I just wanted to see what all was going on today and make sure you weren't going to try to get out of getting your hair done." Allison said as she came up to the car.

"I told you she watches me with her binoculars," Rose said grinning affectionately at the younger woman.

"Where's your shadows?" Blake said grinning at Allison.

Allison's face turned red as she grinned at Blake, "Well, for your information, Reggie is in the house fixing me some breakfast. Liz and Travis have already headed to town."

"Is he running around your house with nothing but an apron on?" Rose asked grinning.

"Grandma! Really!" Kat said shaking her head, "No offense Allison, but I really don't want a picture of Reggie in my head wearing nothing but an apron on."

"I don't know, I think it would be hilarious," Blake said, "but truthfully I don't want to find out."

"Me neither," Shawn said laughing.

"Well, Shawn and Blake are going to get the food and flowers for me. Everyone else can help with decorating. I am going to pick up the cake and ice cream and I guess I am going to be bullied into getting my hair done." Kat said grinning at her friend.

"You betcha!" Allison said.

Reggie stuck his head out of Allison's door, "Hey everyone. How's everybody doing? Ready to get this party started? By the way Allison, breakfast is done."

"Hey Reggie, what color of apron you got on?" Blake hollered.

"Apron? I'm not wearing any apron," Reggie said with a confused look on his face.

"I'll explain it all to you when I get back inside," Allison said.

"Ok. See everyone later," Reggie hollered shaking his head as he went back inside.

Allison smiled as she watched Reggie go back inside. "I will see you all later, got my breakfast to go eat." She said as she started walking back towards her house.

"I haven't seen her this happy in a long time," Rose said, "It is nice to see you girls happy."

A few minutes later and they were pulling around to the back of Grumpy's Palace. Derek and Megan were already there waiting on them.

"Hi sis. I think you need to take a look at Megan's drawings she did. She has made a plan of what the Conference room should look like. I think she has an excellent idea," Derek said looking at Megan with pride in his eyes.

Megan smiled shyly at Kat, "I hope you don't mind. I got an idea in my head last night so I thought I would put it to paper. You don't have to use it if you don't want to."

"Are you kidding me? I would love to take a look at it," Kat said grinning back at her.

Megan gave her a shy smile and handed Kat her notebook. Kat studied the drawing intently. Several minutes went by as everyone waited on Kat's reaction. Megan kept chewing on her lower lip, obviously nervous about Kat's reaction.

"This will work wonderfully!" Kat said giving Megan a big hug, "Your drawing is very detailed. I can tell you put a lot of thought into it."

Megan looked at the drawing and started explaining where the food should go, how the table decorations were set up and the where the flower arrangements should go. The more she talked the more confident her voice became.

"I love the vases you picked out and the candles. If we put them on the tables like this and then put the food and cake over here, I believe that we will have more freedom to move around without being crowded." Megan said taking a strand of her hair and putting it behind her ear.

"You are right. This makes a lot of sense. Have you ever thought about doing event planning or something like that? I think you would be wonderful at it" Kat said.

Megan smiled at Kat, obviously pleased with her reaction. "Thank you. I was trying to remember what all decorations you had. I have the tables pretty well where we discussed and thought that I remembered what all you had yet to do. Let me know if I am missing anything."

"Nope, looks like you have everything. You even remember the flowers. I almost forgot about them earlier," Kat said laughing. "She is a keeper Derek. You better hang on to this one."

"I plan on it," Derek said engulfing Megan in a big hug.

"When you leave this will give us something to go by," Blake agreed looking over Kat's shoulder at the plans.

"Perfect! Let's get started," Kat said grinning.

CHAPTER THIRTY-EIGHT

The day flew by quickly with them all pitching in. Kat and Shawn left and got the cake, which had turned out perfect. Before she knew it, it was time for the girls to head out to get their hair done. After the guys reassured her and more or less pushed her out the door, Kat relented and got Megan and Rose loaded up in her car.

Allison and Liz were waiting on them when they pulled into the parking lot. Lisa gave them all hugs when they walked into her shop.

"I am so happy to see you all. It has been too long, especially you," Lisa said pointing at Kat, "You need to start coming in more regularly."

Kat sighed, "I know, you might as well jump on the band wagon and growl at me too."

"She may start coming in more often," Rose said grinning, "She has her a man now."

"Really! That is wonderful news," Lisa said clapping her hands.

Kat felt her face grow warm, "Grandma! You all act like I've never been in a relationship before." She quickly changed the subject. "We need to get done Lisa; we have a lot more stuff to do."

"Ok, honey," Lisa said winking at her, "Chase, Julie, Tammy-I need your help in here."

Three people came out of the other room. Julie was a petite lady with dark red hair that contained black highlights. Tammy was tall and blond and seemed to always be smiling. Chase was a young man, who this time had purple hair; they never knew what color of hair he was going to have.

"Megan, so nice to see you again. Come with me and we will get you all fixed up." Julie said taking Megan by the hand and leading her into the back room.

"Miss Rose, you are mine honey!" Chase said grinning at the elderly lady.

"Hello handsome," Rose said returning his smile. "You know, I would be trying to rob the cradle if you liked boobs instead of balls."

Chase started laughing, "If I ever decide to like boobs honey, I will let you know."

Lisa motioned for Kat to follow her. "You don't think I'm gonna let you off that easily after hearing you have a man," Lisa teased her.

"I didn't figure I would get off that easy," Kat said returning the woman's smile.

"That leaves you two," Tammy said coming over to Allison and Liz, "Both of you follow me I'm good enough that I can get both of you done."

"No doubt about it," Allison chuckled as they followed her to the back.

"Ok, spill it." Lisa said to Kat as she lathered her hair up.

"What is there to spill? I am seeing a friend of Blake's." Kat said nonchalantly.

"Who happens to be living in her house," Rose hollered.

"Oh honey, there sounds like there is a lot to spill!" Lisa said.

Kat grimaced, "I forgot that once you have a life every one wants to know what your doing all the time!"

"Well, we are here to remind you of that fact. Tell us how this man got you out of your shell." Tammy said smiling as she worked on Allison. Liz was sitting in the chair next to her waiting her turn.

"I really don't know how it happened. I have felt comfortable with him since I first met him. He is laid back and does not expect me to give him more than what I am ready to give. He cooks and picks up after himself. He is even helping me with the construction of the grill." Kat said closing her eyes as Lisa's fingers made the tension go away. "You know, I am not the only one with a man. Reggie and Allison have been spending a lot of time together. He was fixing her breakfast when I picked up Grandma this morning."

"Oh no you don't!" Allison said, "Don't you try to get the conversation on me so that you are left alone."

"I want the juicy stuff," Chase said, "Wait a minute, is the guy you are seeing the one with the dark hair and beautiful blue eyes? If so, I am jealous. He is extremely yummy looking."

"That is the one," Rose said, "Can you believe she hasn't tapped that yet! I would have no time for anything else if I was with someone as fine as he is. Why back in my day, we would..."

"Oh no, please do not give us any of your sex stories," Allison groaned. "We are all having a good time and I don't think these ladies want us throwing up in their sinks."

"I could give you all pointers! You should listen to what I have to tell you. Kat, it has been so long for you that you may need my advice. I would hate for that "yummy" man to move on just because you have forgot how to rock a man's world."

"I love you Miss Rose!" Chase said, "You always brighten my day. I would love to hear more of your sex stories."

"Of course, you would dear, but some of it won't help you any. You don't have the right equipment in some areas and you have too much equipment in others." Rose said.

The women all laughed at Rose's comment. They spent the next 30 minutes chit chatting about different things. Lisa got them all talking about the party and promised to see them later that evening once they were all finished.

The ladies all stopped at their houses to grab their party clothes and met at Rose's house to finish getting ready before heading back to Grumpy's Palace.

"WOW!" Shawn blurted out upon seeing Kat, "You look amazing. I didn't think it would be possible for you to get any more beautiful."

Kat smiled at him; she had to agree with him. She had chosen an emerald green low-cut blouse with a pair of black dress pants. The green of the blouse made the green in her eyes stand-out. Lisa had put all of her hair on the top part of her head but had allowed several curls to remain loose. She hadn't planned on wearing any make-up but Megan had put a little bit on her which only emphasized her green eyes and long lashes. She had completed her outfit with a silver necklace that had an emerald green cross on it with matching earrings and black flats.

"Thank you, kind sir, your words are very much appreciated," Kat said.

"We are heading out to get the food. We will be back soon. Don't let any Prince Charming's come and sweep you off your feet while I'm gone." Shawn teased her.

"You're the only Prince Charming for me," Kat said pulling his head down for a kiss.

"Come on you two, you can get a room later. You keep this up and I'm going to get sick," Blake said.

"Come on Shawn; you and Derek need to get moving. We have to go get that food; I'm starving!" Travis said as he headed out the door. Shawn grinned at her again before turning to follow Travis.

"I will be back soon," Derek said to Megan. "You look wonderful but someone has to go with them two to keep them out of trouble."

"I believe that," Megan said laughing.

Megan had chosen a midnight blue one-piece pant suite. It showed off her curves and complimented her skin tone. Her hair had been left down and her curls hung down her back; when she moved it seemed like her hair was dancing.

The girls all went into the Conference room. It had been transformed into a beautiful room. The candles had all been lit and gave a warm glow to the room while the flower arrangements gave the room color and a pleasing fragrance. Kat felt her heart swell with pride looking at what they had accomplished.

"It looks wonderful. The guys followed your plan pretty good Megan," Kat said.

"Yes, they did. It looks wonderful," Megan said.

"I don't know why you two sound so surprised. After all, I was in charge of following Megan's plan and you know I wouldn't do anything but make everything perfect." Blake said smugly.

"Good grief," Kat said as both her and Megan groaned at Blake's comment.

"I am going to run to my office really quick. I'll be back in a jiffy," Kat said.

"I'll walk with you hon. I have to go to the little girl's room," Rose said grabbing Kat's arm.

"You have done a great job Kathryn. I'm proud of you," Rose said squeezing her granddaughter's arm.

"Thank you, Grandma. It's turning out to be better that I expected. I just hope the rest of the night goes well."

"I am sure you have nothing to worry about. If you get done in your office before I get done, wait for me if you don't mind."

"Of course not." Kat said giving her Grandma a quick hug.

Rose went into the lounge while Kat went to her office. She checked her messages and then looked at her calendar to make sure she had not forgotten anything. Seeing that everything was good and none of the messages on her machine were important, Kat walked out of her office and right into a man that was standing outside her office door.

"Oh, sorry!" Kat said glancing up. "Wait a minute, I know

you. You're the jackass from the restaurant. The one that gave me the note."

"And you're the bitch who hit me with a tray and got me fired," Pete said.

"I didn't get you fired. I thought your manager gave you another chance," Kat said looking at him uneasily.

"They had more complaints about me. Just a bunch of teasing whores like you," he snarled at her.

"Stupid question…. how can a whore be a tease? If she's teasing someone then it is because someone paid her to do it, right?" Kat said attempting to keep him talking. Surely someone would come around the corner soon.

Pete looked confused and then angry. "Shut up! I came here looking for the old lady. She's the real reason all of this happened."

"Why are you blaming her? You're the dumbass who gave a customer, who you didn't even know, a sexual harassing note. The only thing she did that was stupid was try to set me up with someone at a restaurant, which by the way was not you!" Kat said, her temper getting the best of her.

She noticed movement over Pete's shoulder and tried not to give anything away. Apparently, it worked because he didn't give any indication that he saw her glance over his shoulder.

"Because she came into the kitchen and dragged me out wanting me to apologize to you. If she hadn't done that it wouldn't have excavated like it did."

"Excavated? Do you mean escalated?" Kat snorted, "If you don't know what a word means then don't use it. If I was you,

I wouldn't try to use big words because you are just going to strain your brain."

Over Pete's shoulder, she noticed her Grandma put a finger to her lips and walk slowly and steadily back toward the bar. Again, Kat worried that Pete would notice her glancing over his shoulder. She shouldn't have worried herself; he was too busy complaining about women in general.

"All of you are the same. You all think that you are better than men. Well, I've got news for you, you're all worthless. The only thing you are good for is pleasing us men and having brats," Pete said spraying spit everywhere, including on Kat.

"Watch it dickhead! I don't want your germs on me," Kat said, "And you can't say women are worthless and then give examples of what we can do you idiot-that is just contradicting yourself." Kat took a couple steps backwards away from Pete.

"Where do you think you are going? You're not going anywhere," Pete said lunging toward her and grabbing her arm. He reached into his pants pocket and pulled out a switchblade.

Kat immediately stopped struggling.

"You just had to be difficult didn't you. Now look what you made me do. I didn't want to get this out. I was hoping you would constipate so I wouldn't have to make you do what I want," Pete said as his hand tightened on her arm.

"Constipate? You mean cooperate?" Kat couldn't help mumbling.

Pete jerked her hard, pulling her towards him. He put the blade against her throat. "Go ahead, smart something else off and see what happens."

A sound from behind her had both of them looking. Blake had come in the back door and the sound they heard was the door shutting behind him.

When Pete saw Blake, he pulled Kat in front of him and pressed the knife into her neck once again.

"Don't come any closer big guy or I will cut her."

"Sis, this your new man? Are you role playing or what?" Blake said holding his hands up. "Don't let me interfere. I'll just go on back outside."

"Is that how you got in? Through the back entrance? Kat asked him in a neutral voice; she was afraid to get him more wound up than he already was.

"Yes, it is. You think you are so smart. You've had people coming in and out all day. I'm surprised you haven't asked me how I found your bar. The old lady told Matt about the party you were planning and invited him. I overheard and wrote the date and the bar's name down. I had different plans then. I didn't know you were going to get me fired," Pete said smugly although his voice had raised a bit on the last sentence. He had relaxed a bit and had moved the knife away from her throat.

Blake took a step back, "Like I said I will just leave you two alone. You can go back to whatever kinky role playing you were doing. In fact, I might want to suggest you add dancing to your role playing. Kat is a great dancer. Why don't you teach the boy how to dance? Maybe start with the two-step," Blake said raising his eyebrows on the last two words.

Pete smiled at Blake and said, "I already know how to dance. In fact, I could probably teach her a thing or two." He let go of Kat and did a little dance move. When he let go of her, Kat turned and stomped on his foot.

Pete let out a yell, dropped the knife and swung at Kat, knocking her to the ground.

"Boy, you went and messed with the wrong family," Rose said from behind him before hitting him in the head with a glass beer bottle. "I told you I would lay the smack down on you if you ever touched my granddaughter again," she said and then kicked Pete in the stomach after he crumpled to the floor.

Blake quickly went to Pete and kicked the knife away. Pete was laying on the ground with blood running down his face.

"You going to be ok sis? He whopped you a good one," Blake asked Kat, concern in his voice. "By the way, Granny, why didn't you get a beer bottle with beer in it? Why did you use an empty one?"

"Well, it started full but I wasn't going to waste it on this moron. I drunk it while I was waiting on you to distract him," Rose said as she hurried over to Kat to help her up.

"I'll be ok, might have to put ice on my face but at least I didn't get stabbed. Glad you were thinking about not wasting your beer while I was entertaining our guest," Kat added sarcastically looking at her Grandma.

"I am so glad you are not hurt too bad Kathryn. When I seen him talking to you, I went back into the bar and told Leon and Blake what was going on. Blake said he was going outside and was going to come in the back entrance. He wanted Leon to come from the bar and get him while Blake was distracting him and I was supposed to call the cops."

"You can see how that went. I went to grab my ball bat that I keep under the bar and she grabbed a beer bottle and headed this way. You must have chugged that beer to have it drained by the time you hit boy genius here with it," Leon said motioning to the groaning man lying on the floor. He walked over to Kat and turned her face, "Better go get some ice on that kiddo."

Pete groaned again and started to get to his knees. Rose walked over to him and kicked him in the stomach again making him crumble back to the ground.

"If I was you, I would stay on the ground. You don't want to wind my Granny up anymore than you already have. If of course, you decide to get back up, I will not stop you. It would be fun to watch you get your butt kicked by an old lady. I must warn you, if you try to hit her back, I do believe I would have to lay the smack down on you. Be grateful that Granny got to you before I did," Blake said with fire in his eyes.

Derek, Megan, Travis and Shawn all came running toward them from the bar area. "What is going on? Kat what happened to your face? Who is this guy on the floor and why is Grandma kicking him?" All four of them were firing questions at the small group.

Kat let Shawn pull her into the comfort of his arms She cringed a little bit when she laid her head against him. She let out a sigh and then filled them all in on what had transpired.

"You sure your ok, Kat? Maybe you should go to the Emergency Room just in case," Shawn said with worry in his voice.

"I'm not going to the ER. Let's just talk to the cops and then get back to the party. Mom and Dad should be here soon."

"Miss Rose, what did you do now?" Deputy Anderson and a couple other officers were heading their way, "Who is your friend on the ground?"

"I didn't do anything!" Rose said.

"The old lady attacked me," Pete said struggling to his knees.

"Hey look!" Rose shouted. Everyone in the area all looked to where she was pointing. Rose took that opportunity to walk up to Pete and kick him in the stomach again. "Oh no you don't! Stay down you mongrel!"

"Now Miss Rose, maybe you should go on into the other room," Deputy Anderson said.

"I am going to the lounge to get some ice on my face. Come on Grandma. If you need me, you know where I'm at" Kat said. She stayed in the comfort of Shawn's arms as they headed to the lounge.

Kat sank into a chair at one of the tables as Shawn got a baggy and put ice in it. He wrapped it in one of the towels that was laying on the counter and gently put it against her face.

Kat hadn't been sitting very long when she heard a loud commotion out in the hall.

"Your telling me that piece of shit over there is the one that threatened my daughter?" Kat heard her Mom's voice; she sighed, so much for the surprise party.

Her parents rushed into the lounge followed by Grant.

"Sorry Kat, they heard about this on the scanner and there was no way I was going to keep them away," Grant said.

"You ok baby?" her Mom asked coming over to Kat's side. "What the heck is going on and what happened to your face?"

Kat told the story again. Her parents would interrupt her with questions or loud exclamations. When her parents heard that Pete had held a knife to Kat's throat, her Dad jumped up and headed for the door.

"I'm going to kill that S.O.B!"

Kat's Mom got up to go after her husband, "Not if I get to him first!" she said.

Derek popped his head into the lounge, "How you feeling sis?"

"Don't worry about me right now, go stop Mom and Dad from killing Pete!" Kat exclaimed.

Derek didn't hesitate as he turned around and hurried after his parents.

Kat followed Derek after their parents with Rose and Shawn right behind her. Her parents had left the bar and were at their truck. Derek was trying to talk them into putting the gun their Dad had out back into the truck.

Blake and Grant appeared out there and between all of them they were able to talk them into putting the gun back into the truck.

"Come on inside. Kat's been through enough. Let's go have a drink," Rose said ushering everyone back toward the entrance.

"Let's all go into the Conference room, we can have more privacy," Blake suggested winking at Kat.

"Good idea Blake," Kat smiled at her older brother. Maybe they could still have a surprise party.

They all headed into the Conference room. Kat smiled as

she walked in and seen how many people were waiting on her parents.

"Surprise!" everyone yelled as her parents walked in.

Her parents both stopped and gaped, "You kids put this all together for us?"

"Well, it was mostly Kat but yeah, we helped some," Derek said smiling.

Her Mom had tears in her eyes as she hugged her daughter, "We could have lost you tonight," she whispered.

"But you didn't so let's enjoy your party," Kat said smiling.

CHAPTER THIRTY-NINE

Kat shook her head at her Grandma. "I don't know why you don't at least go talk to him. You know you are interested."

"I never said I was interested in him!" Rose snapped, "I don't know what Charlie is doing here anyway."

"You're just saying that because you don't have enough alcohol in your system to admit it yet." Blake said laughing.

"I beg to differ, I believe Grandma has quite a lot of alcohol in her system," Derek said grinning.

Blake and Kat had been giving Rose a hard time ever since Charlie had shown up. Everyone else at the table had enjoyed Rose's obvious discomfort. As soon as he had seen Rose, Charlie had headed in her direction. Rose, on the other hand, had seen him coming her way and had bolted to the women's restroom.

"Too bad Mom's parents couldn't have made it," Blake laughed, "this party would have gotten a lot more interesting."

"It is too bad they couldn't make it but with Grandma being that sick they didn't need to be doing any travelling."

"I wonder why Grandpa didn't just show up and leave Grandma at home?" Blake mused, "Oh wait, I know, she probably didn't want him around Granny here. For some odd reason, she just doesn't trust you!" Blake laughed as he finished his beer.

"Not my fault that she is no fun and I look better in her

clothes that she does," Rose snorted.

"I'm going to get me another beer. Anyone need anything?" Blake asked as he stood his long frame up.

"Well, just as long as you're going up there, you can grab me one, son," Blake's father said coming up behind Blake and smacking him on the back.

"I need another one too, especially if I have to put up with you smart allecs." Rose said.

Blake smiled and shook his head at her as he headed up to the bar.

"Because you just have to have an excuse to have another drink right Mom," Edward said shaking his head at his mother.

"I don't need any sass from you boy. Don't make me get up on this table and do a flying karate kick at your punk ass."

"I'd like to see that," Derek chimed in. For most of the night he had been pretty satisfied with just sitting beside Megan and watching everyone else.

"Don't think I can't do it either," Rose said standing up and shaking her finger in Derek's direction. Edward moved closer to his mother as she swayed back and forth.

"I didn't say you couldn't do it, I just said I wanted to watch you do it. Geez Grandma, don't get your panties up in a bunch," Derek laughed.

"Your darn a-tooting I can do it," Rose said, "And what makes you think I have panties on to get all in a bunch?"

"Not to change the subject, even though you all can thank me later for doing it, but Mom, it is getting pretty late. You want us to take you home? I think I am going to go grab Chey so we can head back to the house. It's been a long day," Edward said letting out an exaggerated yawn.

"I'm not so sure I am ready to go yet. Besides, you two can't leave your own party this early. All these people came here to see you two," Rose said giving her son a disapproving look, "The kids, especially Kat, put a lot of their time into this party. Kat even got held at knife point by that stupid punk."

"I'm fine Grandma," Kat said. Her face was showing the sign of bruising but she was snuggled up against Shawn with a big grin on her face. "Besides a lot of people have already left. The party started five hours ago. I am sure we will be kicking people out of here before much longer. If Mom and Dad are ready to leave and you want to go with them, I'm sure the rest of us will be leaving right behind you."

"Here's your beer Dad," Blake said coming up to their table, "Here Granny, since you are a lush, I figured you might be having withdrawals if I didn't bring you your drink," he said as he put her drink in front of her.

"Thanks Blake. I think I'll finish this beer and head home. Mom, once you finish your drink, we will take you on home," Edward said as he picked up his beer and took a long drink.

"You don't be telling me when I am going home. I'll go home when I am good and ready," Rose grumbled as she sat back down at the table and took a drink.

"You are going home when we leave even if I have to throw you over my shoulder," Edward said.

"Now honey, don't talk to your Mom that way," Cheyenne said coming up behind her husband and wrapping her arms around him.

"She is going home when we go home; she's drunk," Edward said "I'm just taking care of her."

"So are you dear," Cheyenne reminded her husband.

"That's why you are driving my sweet little honeybun," Edward said pulling his wife around to give her a kiss.

"Edward James, I am your Mother and you better remember that before you start mouthing," Rose said as she made an attempt to stand up only to fall back onto her seat.

"Grandma, all of us are going home," Kat said soothingly as she leaned toward her Grandma and put a hand on her arm, "Since we are all going home it's probably a good thing if you go with us; otherwise, how are you getting home?"

"Unless you want Charlie to take you home and get you all tucked in," Blake said with a grin.

"I'm surrounded by a bunch of smart asses. I'm not going home with any of you and I sure the hell am not going to go home with Charlie. I'll call me a cab!" Rose growled.

"Ok, that's it Mom; I'm done being the loving son," Edward said as he stood up after downing the rest of his beer. "Up you go," he said as he pulled her chair away from the table. He easily lifted Rose up and threw her over his wide shoulder.

Rose started hollering at her son to put her down which was soon followed by a string of words that would make a sailor blush.

"Night everyone," Edward said as he headed for the door.

"Edward, be careful with her," Cheyenne said as her husband

staggered a bit.

"Well crap," Kat said, "I better go out there to make sure everything goes well. The last time they got into it, Grandma threw rocks at Dad and busted the window out of his truck!"

"You all come by your scrappiness honestly, don't you," Shawn said smiling at Kat as he got up to follow her out. He was followed by Derek, Megan and Blake.

Rose was still hollering and swearing as she laid over her son's shoulder. "Put me down you ungrateful jackass!"

"Fine," Edward said as he put his Mom down on the ground.

Cheyenne hurried by them to unlock the doors on their truck.

"Grandma we are all leaving, see," Kat said motioning to everyone.

Rose looked at everyone, "You all suck. This is supposed to be a party and you all are acting like a bunch of senior citizens who are unable to get around anymore."

Blake walked up to his Grandma and offered her his arm, "Want me to help you Grandma?"

"Hell, no I don't want you to help me!" Rose snapped, "I am perfectly capable of getting in the truck without any of you lame, no fun, twerps helping me."

They all watched Rose as she headed to the back of the truck.

"What is she doing?" Derek asked as they watched Rose. She stopped at the tailgate of the truck and started pulling as hard as she could on the bumper and then tried the tail gate.

"What the hell! I thought you were going to unlock the truck doors Cheyenne," Rose said still pulling on the back of the truck.

Blake started laughing and everyone who's mouth was not hanging open soon joined him. Blake was laughing so hard he just sat down in the parking lot.

"Mom, what do you think you are doing? Chey did unlock the doors. Your pulling on the tailgate and the bumper you crazy ole coot!" Edward said.

"Come on Grandma," Kat said hurrying to her Grandma's side, "Let me help you. Mom unlocked the doors over there, you can get in that way."

"Ok, Kat. Thank you for your help," Rose said, all the fight going out of her as she let Kat lead her to the back door of the truck.

Rose obediently got in the truck like she hadn't been acting crazy just moments before.

"Get your butt in the truck Edward," Cheyenne said, "I'm ready to get you both home so I can get some sleep."

"Will they be ok?" Shawn asked as he came to stand beside Kat.

"Sure," Kat said, "This isn't nothing. You should have been here when Grandma threw a fit to ride home in one of the fire trucks," Kat put her arm around Shawn's waste. "It's not too late to make a run for it. Things are never normal around here."

"Who wants normal anyway," Shawn said leaning down and giving her a quick kiss, "Normal is boring. Let's go home. I can't wait to see what tomorrow will be like!"